SPACE
DEMONS

SPACE
DEMONS
GILLIAN RUBINSTEIN

Dial Books for Young Readers
New York

First published in the United States 1988
by Dial Books for Young Readers
A Division of NAL Penguin Inc.
2 Park Avenue
New York, New York 10016

Published simultaneously in Canada by
Fitzhenry & Whiteside Limited, Toronto
First published in Australia 1986
by Omnibus Books, Adelaide, Australia
Copyright © 1986 by Gillian Rubinstein
All rights reserved
Printed in the U.S.A.

COBE
2 4 6 8 10 9 7 5 3

Library of Congress Cataloging in Publication Data
Rubinstein, Gillian.
Space demons / by Gillian Rubinstein.
p. cm.
Summary: Twelve-year-old Andrew, bored with life,
becomes obsessed with a mysterious new
computer game, which has the power to zap him
and his friends into a dangerous world
of menacing space warriors.
ISBN 0-8037-0534-4
[1. Computer games—Fiction. 2. Science fiction.] I. Title.
PZ7.R83133Sp 1988 [Fic]—dc19 87-27542 CIP AC

To Matthew, Tessa, and Susannah

1

Go on, Andrew, try it!" Ben was tired of playing by himself. He knew the sequence of the game too well. It was no longer a challenge playing against the computer. But if two people played against each other, the game was more unpredictable and more fun.

"Not now," Andrew Hayford said. He was lying on his bed leafing through a *Mad* magazine. "I've played it too many times. It's boring." He threw the magazine down on the floor, got off the bed, and walked across to the window. "Everything's boring," he said, looking out moodily at the rain that was sweeping across the gardens and streets outside. "I wish it would stop raining. This winter seems to be going on forever."

"Do you want to do anything else?" Ben asked. A slight, blond-haired boy, he was smaller than Andrew and a few weeks younger. He and Andrew had been best friends in an unquestioning sort of way ever since they had started kindergarten together. They were now in seventh grade.

"There's nothing *to* do!" Andrew said, turning around from the window. The friendship was not an entirely equal one. Ben Challis liked and admired Andrew, but Andrew tended to consider Ben a sort of useful sidekick—he called all the shots and Ben invariably went along with whatever he wanted. As a result, Andrew did not always treat Ben very well. This was one of those times.

"You might as well go home," he said. "Go and play your own games on your own computer."

"I never get a chance to get on it," Ben said. "Darren's always using it. He thinks he's some kind of hacker!" Darren, his brother, was fifteen and in high school. One of the reasons Ben put up with Andrew bossing him around was because he was used to being bossed around by Darren. He got up from the computer. "All the same, I suppose I'd better go. It's getting dark."

"Yeah, you don't want to get mugged between here and Forsyth Avenue!"

There was a slight note of scorn in the way Andrew said this that annoyed Ben. He looked at the other boy and found himself wondering, not for the first time, why they were friends. He shrugged his shoulders, not rising to the bait, and said, "Well, see you at school tomorrow."

"School!" Andrew said in disgust. "Of all the boring things, that has to be the most boring!"

They walked down the stairs together. At the bottom Andrew grinned at Ben, crossed his eyes hideously, and gave him a friendly punch on the shoulder.

Ben grinned back—he could never resent Andrew for

long. No one could. He was an astonishingly good-looking boy, with a charming and confident manner that attracted people effortlessly. An only child, he had never known any hardships or setbacks, and everything came easily to him. He had a cheerful and fearless nature, and he believed the universe existed largely for his benefit. Lately, though, it seemed to be letting him down. He felt as if he were stuck in some sort of limbo: bored with school, no longer a child, not quite a teenager. He was either too old or too young for everything. Books, games, and television programs that six months ago had been exciting now seemed boring and pointless. He had played all the games, read all the books, seen all the programs . . . done everything, and he was still only twelve!

He closed the door behind Ben and walked through the large house to the family room at the back. His mother was in the kitchen that led off it. When she saw Andrew, she called out, "Dinner's ready. Has Ben gone home?"

"Yeah, he just left."

"He was a little late leaving," Marjorie Hayford said, looking out the window. "It's practically dark. I wish he'd get started earlier."

"Mom, he's not going to be abducted between here and Forsyth Avenue!"

"Kids do get abducted, you know," she said, lifting the lid off the casserole she had just taken out of the oven. She poked the meat inside it experimentally with a fork. "I think this is done."

"Yes, I know," Andrew said, leaning over the countertop to smell the casserole, "but not very often, and I can't see it happening to a kid like Ben."

"Why not?" his mother asked.

"I don't know," Andrew said. "He's just a careful type, or something. Are you going to serve that stuff or not, Marjorie?"

"Don't call me Marjorie," she scolded. But secretly she liked it, and she was smiling as she ladled meat and sauce onto his plate. He was such a handsome boy, and so charming. A faint fear crept over her that he was the type that might be abducted. As though he could read her thoughts, he looked up and smiled. "And don't worry about me. I can look after myself." He took a mouthful of food and said, "What time's Dad going to be home?"

Dr. Robert Hayford had been away for a week at a medical conference in Osaka. Andrew had hardly missed him. He never saw very much of him anyway: As far as he was concerned, his father might just as well have lived in Japan. Dr. Hayford worked at a big teaching hospital in the city and was both dedicated and ambitious.

"He should be back soon. He was going to get a taxi from the airport," his mother answered.

"I hope he didn't forget to get me a present," Andrew said.

His father had not forgotten. Practically the first thing he did when he came through the door was to open his briefcase and take out a small package. "Here you are, Andrew!" he said, handing it to his son. "The latest breakthrough from the high-tech Orient. That should keep you quiet for a while."

"Oh, fantastic!" Andrew exclaimed. "Thanks, Dad."

He tore off the wrapping paper eagerly. Inside was a box containing a computer diskette. On the box there was an exciting-looking picture of a spaceman in a shining white suit, back to back with a rather sinister individual dressed entirely in black, with black, spiky hair. From the side of the picture facing the spaceman another figure advanced, similar to the first, except that its hair was cut in a punk-style mohawk. All three characters held cylindrical black weapons from which fiery orange tracers were flashing. Across the picture, in purple and black letters, blazed the words SPACE DEMONS. Down the side and along the bottom were a lot of Japanese characters neither Andrew nor his parents could understand.

"It's excellent," Andrew said in delight. "No one else will have this one! Ben'll go insane!" He looked at it lovingly. It was much more than a present from an overseas trip: It was a status symbol that would arouse envy and admiration in his friends.

"I'll go and try it out right away," he said.

"Have you done your homework?" his mother asked.

"I can do it in the morning," Andrew assured her.

"Aren't you supposed to do your homework before you go on the computer?" his father said.

"I just want to try out the new game, Dad. I haven't got much homework, and I'll get it done in the morning, I promise." Andrew was turning on the full charm, eyes wide open, face alert and smiling.

Is he really aware he does it? his mother thought. Or is it unconscious?

Whichever it was, her husband could no more resist it than she could. "Okay," he said. "That's fine by me, as long as it gets done. You'd better get off to bed good and early, though."

"After I've tried out the game," Andrew said.

His father reached out and ruffled his hair. "Don't stay up too long." The look of pride on his face was replaced by one of annoyance as the click of a lighter and the sharp smell of smoke announced that his wife had lit a cigarette.

"How many have you had today?" he asked. His voice was cold.

"I haven't counted," she answered shortly. "Not more than five or ten."

"Five or ten!" he exploded. "That's a damn sight too many! For heaven's sake, Marjorie, you'd given it up for a year! Why on earth have you started again?"

"I just happen to feel like it," she said. "*You* do things you feel like doing. I don't consider ten cigarettes excessive. I can afford it."

"It's not a question of money," Dr. Hayford retorted. "It's a question of health!"

"I'm perfectly healthy. It doesn't even make me cough."

"You're a doctor's wife!" he said angrily.

Andrew decided it was time to leave the room. They were both talking more loudly than they needed to, and he didn't want to be there when they started shouting. He realized with a feeling of dismay that the week his father had been away had been peaceful—there had been no arguments, and his mother had been relaxed and happy. As soon as his father had walked into the house, tension had walked in with him.

He went up the stairs thinking about this, but by the time he reached his room he had decided to forget it. He looked instead at the box in his hands. It promised to be something exciting. He opened it and took out the diskette. "You'd better be good!" he said to it.

He was in for a disappointment. There were no instructions in English, and Andrew couldn't work out what the point of the game was. It looked beautiful enough. The screen was a brilliant shade of blue, and a wonderfully shiny space rocket rose from the earth toward distant stars. Moving the joystick to the right made the boosters detach and fall away, and then the little cone-shaped module that remained sailed off the screen. The process repeated itself. Nothing Andrew did made anything else happen at all.

He heard a door bang downstairs and then heavy footsteps on the stairs. His father stood in the doorway of his room. "What's it like?" he asked.

Andrew turned toward him, instantly noticing and deciding not to notice at the same time that his father's face was hard and angry. "I don't get it," he said. "It seems really weak—and yet I'm sure it's not. It must do more than just this."

"Professor Ito said it was the prototype of a new sort of game—something he's developing for fun. I think I told you before what a genius he is. He said it was a bit tricky to get the hang of, but he thought you'd be interested in taking a shot. I told him you were an expert."

"You try it," Andrew offered. "See what you make of it."

"I haven't got time right now," his father said. "I've got a couple of phone calls to make, and then I must get some sleep. It's been an exhausting week, and the flight was pretty tiring too. I'll have a look at it later, okay?"

He smiled as he said it, but the smile could not mask the rejection. Andrew did not really mind: He had not expected anything else. "Okay," he said, going back to the game.

He tried to consider the problem logically. You must have to do something to extend the game or get a new screen, he thought. And since the only thing I've got any control over is when the boosters fire, it must be something to do with that.

He tried firing them at several different points as the space rocket soared diagonally across the screen, but the degree of accuracy was not great enough. Engrossed in the problem now, he took off his digital watch and put it in front of him on the computer, setting the seconds to flash. He went through the game again, firing the booster after one second, after two seconds, after three. When he got to six his efforts were rewarded. As the boosters fell away, the game gave a high-pitched shriek, the screen changed to violet, and asteroids of deep purple, mauve, and amethyst began to bombard the silver space module.

Evasion was the only defense. The module responded accurately to the joystick, but it did not seem to have any means of destroying the asteroids. After several attempts, however, Andrew found that the asteroid bombardment followed a set pattern, and he could avoid destruction for longer and longer periods, getting higher and higher scores. It was quite entertaining, and he loved the moment when the violet screen flashed up and the silver module stood out against all the different shades of purple, but he felt there must be still more to the game. So far it had not been very different from dozens of other games he had played—and where were the promised space demons?

He was now scoring 8,000 or more. Downstairs the phone rang. Gee, he thought, Dad's just come back from overseas and they can't leave him alone for a moment. I'll never be a doctor when I grow up. He heard the TV being turned down, and his mother called up to him, "Andrew! Bedtime!"

"Okay," he shouted back. But to himself he said, "I'll just try for 10,000 before I go to bed."

He didn't have to get to 10,000. Not quite. Watching the score out of the corner of his eye as he kept the module dodging the asteroids, he saw it reach 9,876. At that moment the screen flashed three times. Almost as if it's winking, Andrew thought, and he had a brief, chilling impression of the intelligence behind the game.

The screen changed color again, violet giving way to pink. The asteroids were exploding, and the fragments were turning into something else—into little figures with black weapons in their hands. They came pouring across the screen like alien and menacing insects. Before Andrew had time to maneuver the module out of their way, they blew it apart in a red and orange flash, and the deep blue of the original screen returned.

It had all happened so quickly that he could hardly believe he had seen them. He sat and gazed at the screen, amazed. He had a feeling that this was still only the beginning of the game. Now that he had seen the space demons he could not wait to see them again and to find out what happened next. Excitement hit him like a fist in the pit of his stomach, making him grin, making his eyes sparkle. Life suddenly seemed much more interesting. He reset his watch and began to play Space Demons again.

The day after Andrew Hayford's father had brought Space Demons back from Japan, Elaine Taylor was doing the splits on the floor of her room. Not *her* room, but the room she was sleeping in, just as it was not *her* house but the house she and her father were living in. Even her clothes—lying in piles on the floor, since the only piece of furniture in the room was a bed—were not *her* clothes but thrift-shop bargains and hand-me-downs from friends. She rolled over on her stomach and bent her back until her feet touched her head. Owning anything new is against Dad's principles, she thought bitterly, looking at the clothes. Upside down they looked shabbier than ever. The only thing that was all hers and that she could feel proud of was her own body. She sat up and put her right foot behind her neck. Ouch! She was a bit stiff this morning. With all the excitement of moving into a new place, she had skipped her workout session for a couple of days, and her muscles were complaining.

"Elaine!" her father shouted from the end of the house. "I've put the kettle on. Do you want a cup of cocoa before you go?"

She unwound herself and shouted back, "Yes, I'm coming!" Getting up from the floor, she put on a sweater, jeans, and sneakers, pulled her hair free from the sweatband that had been holding it back from her face, and twisted it into a single braid that hung down her back almost to her waist.

"I think I'll get my hair cut," she said when she got to the kitchen.

"What for?" her father said. "It's nice." He had the same sort of hair: dark red, thick and wavy. His was long, too, down to his shoulders, and he had a lighter, sandy beard.

"It gets in my way when I'm working out."

David Taylor shrugged his broad shoulders. "It's your hair," he said. "Cut it if you want to. It'll always grow again."

Typical, she thought to herself. He never minds at all.

He doesn't mind about anything. Nothing I do matters to him. She studied him critically as he made his tea. The tea bag looked tiny in his huge hand. Ginger hairs grew thickly up his arms, curling around the red-and-blue tattoo that disappeared under the sleeve of his sweatshirt. Most of the time she accepted him unconditionally as her dad, and loved him, but now and then she saw him from a distance, with a stranger's eyes, and he worried and irritated her.

Boy, what a hulk! she thought. I'm not surprised Mom took off! I wish I could.

He swung the tea bag deftly from the cup to the sink and looked across at her. "What're you dreaming about, Elly?"

"Oh, nothing," she said, with a twinge of guilt. They never talked about her mother, who two years ago had suddenly disappeared. Her absence left a great hole in Elaine's life, like a spiked trap dug in the ground: Most of the time she could circle successfully around it, but occasionally she stumbled into it, to be impaled yet again.

It would have been easier if her father had talked to her about it. But whenever she tried to mention it, he clamped his lips together, and later he would lose his temper with her, apparently over something else. The silence filled her with pain and guilt, and the anger with fear and resentment. Because she had nobody to talk to about the way she felt, she wrote endless letters to her mother in her head. Most of them never got written down, and the ones that actually did get written were never mailed—she did not know where to send them—but they gave her the illusion that her mother was still within reach and still cared for her.

Dear Mom, she now wrote in her mind, *I've got to go to*

another new school. I need some new clothes. And do you think I should get my hair cut?

She sat down at the table and took the mug of cocoa her father pushed toward her. A few moments earlier she had been complaining that nothing she did mattered to him. Now, perversely, it gave her a feeling of satisfaction that he had no idea what was going on inside her head. She stirred the cocoa, looking around at the half-built kitchen. On the table were some slices of bread, a container of margarine, and a jar of jam. Both the margarine and the jam had flecks of sawdust in them.

"You want something to eat?" her father asked, putting down his cup and helping himself to bread and jam and sawdust.

Elaine shook her head. "I'm not hungry."

"Suit yourself." He got up, still chewing. "I'd better get to work. There's a heck of a lot to do on this place, and we don't want to stay here forever."

"Aren't you coming up to the school with me?" she asked quickly.

He looked at her in surprise. "Do you want me to?"

"Yeah," she said, but in fact she wasn't sure. He was so noticeable, that was the trouble. People always stared at him: He was so big, and he had so much red hair. But going to a new school alone was dreadful too.

It didn't matter that she couldn't decide. Her father had already decided. He picked up the power saw that was lying on the half-finished workbench.

"You'll be all right," he said. "I'll meet you up there afterward, okay?"

"Okay," she replied. "Can I have some money for lunch?"

He took two dollars out of his pocket and gave it to her. "Have a good day, kiddo!"

"Okay," she said again. The noise of the saw started up before she had opened the front door and let herself out.

Dear Mom, she thought, beginning a new letter as the door banged shut behind her, *Not only is your daughter going to a new school with no new clothes, she is also going with no breakfast. In the rain,* she added as she dodged the wet, tangled shrubs in the overgrown garden and went out past a front gate that had fallen off its hinges and now leaned against a crumbling stone wall.

As she stepped onto the pavement, a bicycle raced past her and jumped off the curb, splashing her feet and legs with water. She caught sight of a dark-haired boy in a black jacket and black jeans, and she yelled after him, "Watch where you're going, you idiot!"

Another boy came out of the driveway of the house next door, shouting, "Wait for me, Mars! Mom said you should wait for me!"

The boy on the bike took no notice of either of them, and disappeared around the corner. His brother gave a theatrical sigh, muttering to himself, "Wait till I tell Mom." He had a round, olive-skinned face, cheerful and plump, with brown hair and eyes.

"Hey," he said to Elaine. "Did you just move in?"

"Yeah."

"You going to Kingsgate School? I'll walk along with you, show you the way."

"I can find it myself," she said warily. She had started new schools so often that she had grown careful. It didn't pay to be too friendly with anyone to start with. Usually the kids who went out of their way to be friendly were the ones nobody else liked. They cornered you, and then nobody else wanted to know you.

"What's your name?" the boy asked, unsnubbed. Elaine

realized that he would be hard to shake off. He was about as sensitive as a jackhammer. "Elaine Taylor," she said, with a slight upward inflection, meaning, "You want to make something of it?"

"Mine's John," he said. "John Ferrone. We live next door to you. That was my brother, Mario. He's supposed to wait for me, but he never does. He's in the ninth grade and I'm in the seventh. What are you?"

"Seventh," she said. This time the inflection meant "Mind your own business." She started walking quickly up the road.

John Ferrone walked along next to her, wheeling his bicycle. "Did you really pay a fortune for the house?" he said. "My dad says you were taken for a ride."

"We didn't pay anything for it," Elaine said. "It doesn't belong to us. We're just staying in it for a while."

"I didn't think your dad could've afforded it. He's a carpenter, isn't he? I saw the pickup with all his tools."

Snoopy kid, Elaine thought angrily.

"He's fixing the house up, isn't he?" John didn't exactly ask questions, he made statements, and if you didn't answer them, he assumed they were true. Now he made another one. "Your mom's not around. She dead?"

Dear Mom, Elaine thought, *Are you dead? Is that why you never answer my letters?*

"No," she said aloud, "she's not dead. She's in the city."

"She run out on you?" John asked.

Elaine did not answer. John observed a few seconds of silence in sympathy, and then started again. "Were you with a circus?"

This surprised her so much that she turned to face him. "Why?"

"I've seen you doing those gymnastics. You're really

good. And your dad looks like a circus type—he could be a weightlifter. And he's got long hair too."

"We traveled with a circus for a while," she said. "A couple of years ago." Immediately she wished she hadn't admitted it. She was angry with this boy who had already discovered so many of her secrets.

"Wish I could do that stuff," he was saying. "You know anything else? Any magic tricks? I love magic tricks. Or juggling?"

Elaine pressed her lips closer together so she wouldn't say anything. In fact her father could juggle, knew a lot of magic tricks, and loved showing them to people, but if she told John that, he'd be coming around all the time. She walked faster. John got on his bike and pedaled slowly along beside her. He didn't ask her any more questions. Instead he told her about himself. She heard about his three brothers, one married with a baby daughter and living out of town, one still living at home but working, and Mario, the wild fourteen-year-old, whom John alternately feared and admired. By the time they got to the school gate Elaine knew all about his mother, a hospital nurse who worked long hours, and his father, who was a builder. She also knew that if she didn't get rid of John Ferrone soon, she would go bananas.

John had no intention of being ditched. "Come on," he said, as they walked into the schoolyard. "There's Mr. Russell, our teacher. We'll ask if I can be your partner. Everyone new gets a partner to keep an eye out for them the first week at school."

Oh, no, thought Elaine. Everything's going wrong! I'm going to be stuck with this creep, and I don't see any other girls wearing jeans!

Mr. Russell was young and friendly. "Hi, Elaine," he said. "You're in my seventh-grade class. I'll show you where the classroom is and get you some books. Thanks, John, but I think we'll find one of the girls to look after Elaine. You go and put your bike away in the rack."

All right, thought Elaine. This teacher knows what's going on. He'd be a hard one to fool.

Mr. Russell walked fast, and she trotted along next to him, trying to check out as much of the school as she could. Most of the buildings were new and modern, painted in bright, primary colors, and there were large grassy areas with playground equipment—climbing apparatus and monkey bars—that made her eyes gleam. Mr. Russell was asking her questions about her last school and telling her that at Kingsgate she was expected to wear a uniform. If she had any problems, she was to go to the office and they would help her.

Problems! she thought to herself. No problems. Just Dad! How do I explain him to the office!

When they got to the classroom, which was in a prefab building on the edge of the school grounds, Mr. Russell flung open the door with vigor, and a girl inside jumped like a startled rabbit.

"Linda!" he said sharply. "What are you doing in here?"

She gave him a guilty smile and looked down at a piece of paper on which she had been writing. "Oh, nothing," she answered.

"You know the rules, Linda. You stay outside until you hear the bell."

"Sorry, Mr. Russell," she said. She gave him another smile, not so guilty this time, more dazzling.

Disarmed by it, Mr. Russell said, "Well, since you're

here, you can do something useful for me. You can be Elaine's partner. Make sure she knows what to do and feels at home. There's an empty desk in front of you, isn't there? Where Cathy Clements used to sit? Elaine can sit there. I'll go and get her books now." He raced off toward the staff room, leaving the two girls looking at each other.

Neither was very impressed by what she saw. They could hardly have been more different. Elaine, skinny and pale in her jeans and sweater, looked untidy and almost wild, her dark red hair already escaping from her not very efficient braid. Linda's blond hair was cut in a fashionable style, and she had an air of being very well cared for. Her clothes were neat and new and her shoes were polished. All of her looked polished, in fact: polished and cherished. Both girls felt vaguely threatened, and their reaction to each other was guarded and hostile.

Linda sat coolly at her desk again and continued writing on the piece of paper, smiling to herself. Her desk was covered with little gadgets—four different self-inking stamps, a pink pencil holder, and a little plastic chest of drawers, also pink, filled with erasers. Tiny photographs, cut from a class photo, were taped to the desktop, and an elaborately designed and colored label announced, LINDA SCHULZ SITS HERE. Elaine studied all these things in silence.

Linda finished writing and folded the note. She crossed the room and placed it on top of a desk in the back row. "Don't you dare tell anyone," she said to Elaine. "That was a note to Andrew Hayford. He's my boyfriend." And you'd better stay away from him, her tone clearly implied.

Because she was feeling put down, Elaine sounded nastier than she meant to. "I couldn't care less," she said. "I'm not interested in that stuff."

Linda didn't need to say, "No, I don't suppose you are." Her scornful look and half smile said it for her.

"Well, are you coming?" she said. "I suppose I'd better show you around before the bell rings."

3

Andrew reached into the back of the Volvo and took out his knapsack. "See you, Mom," he said quickly.

"I'll pick you up after school, it might be raining," she said.

"Okay." He could tell by her tone of voice that she was in a good mood. It was worth a try. "Can I have some money?" he asked.

"What happened to your allowance?"

"I spent it all on Saturday," he said cheerfully.

"I haven't got any change," his mother said. "If I give you five dollars you'll have to make it last."

"Five dollars will be fine! Thanks, Mom!"

Andrew swaggered into the schoolyard. Five dollars in his pocket made him feel as though he owned the whole school. He went to look for Ben. Ben's parents were both teachers so he was usually at school early, hanging around the entrance waiting for Andrew, who was usually late. This morning there was no sign of him, which was annoying because Andrew was longing to tell him about the game his father had brought from Japan. I wonder if Ben'll be able to work out Space Demons, he thought. I won't tell him what I've found out so far. I'll see if he can get it.

He tracked Ben down at last, among a group of students outside the seventh-grade classroom. They were watching a redheaded girl whom Andrew had never seen before, walking on her hands on the grass.

"Hey, what's going on?" Andrew asked. Ben turned around and gave him a grin, but it was John Ferrone, standing next to him, who answered. "It's the new girl, Elaine Taylor. She used to be in a circus."

"What was she, the trained chimpanzee?" Andrew snorted. He felt vaguely irritated that anyone else should be the center of attention.

Linda Schulz heard him and laughed. She came over and stood next to him. "What a show-off!" she said. "Her first morning at school, and look at her!"

Ignoring Linda, Andrew pulled Ben aside. He was busy telling him about Space Demons when the bell rang and everyone ran to line up.

Elaine turned herself right-side up. She was furious with herself. She hadn't meant to show off, but somehow it always happened. The more nervous and out of place she felt, the more she seemed to have to draw attention to herself. Linda had been so stuck-up and nasty as she showed her around the school, that when they got back to the grass, Elaine hadn't been able to resist the urge to show what she could do. So while Linda was in mid-sentence, she had suddenly done a forward somersault in the air without using her hands, and then a series of back flips. Other students had gathered around to watch, and she had found she couldn't stop. Now her hands were muddy from the wet grass, and she had managed to get mud smeared on her face.

Mr. Russell came up and cast his eye over the waiting group, frowning slightly when he saw Elaine. He was pleased with the way things were going in his class: He felt that he and the students understood and respected each other, and that they had a good relationship. He very much hoped this new girl was not going to disrupt that.

"You look rather muddy, Elaine," he said. "Linda, show Elaine where to wash her hands, please."

"He likes us to look neat," Linda said as they walked toward the washroom. On their way back she said, "Andrew said you looked like a chimpanzee."

"Oh, did he?" Elaine said. "He sounds like a pain in the neck."

I wonder which one he is, she thought as they entered the classroom. The rest of the class was turning to page eighty-eight in *Mathematics and Real Life*, while Mr. Russell was writing on the blackboard. Most of the students stared at Elaine, and a boy in the back row made a monkey face at her by putting his tongue behind his bottom lip and crossing his eyes. She could feel Linda next to her trying not to laugh. Aha, thought Elaine, that must be the famous Andrew. Very funny!

Mr. Russell turned around. "I'd like you all to meet our new class member," he said. "This is Elaine Taylor. I hope you'll make her feel at home at Kingsgate."

Elaine felt herself going pink. She wiggled her ears. She really didn't mean to, it just sometimes happened when she was embarrassed. She hoped Mr. Russell hadn't noticed. But half the class had. They stared at her in fascination, wondering if she would do it again.

"You can sit down now, Elaine," Mr. Russell said. His voice sounded cool.

He *did* notice, she thought. She sat down quickly and

kept her eyes firmly down in case she did anything else
stupid.

As Mr. Russell turned to write on the board again, Elaine
felt something hit her on the foot. She looked down and
saw a paper airplane on the floor. Linda, behind her, was
trying to reach it with a ruler. Forgetting all her good
intentions, Elaine bent down swiftly and picked it up.

"Give it to me," Linda hissed.

Elaine's behavior often surprised even herself. She knew
all the unwritten rules about being new at school—act like
a new person, don't show off, let everyone boss you
around—but somehow she was unable to keep them. So
she didn't give the airplane back to Linda. Instead she
picked it up, opened it, read what was on it, and gave a
very realistic but perfectly silent imitation of someone
being sick.

Linda reached forward to grab the piece of paper, and
Elaine, keeping an eye on Mr. Russell at the blackboard,
let her take it. Mr. Russell turned around at the exact
moment when Linda, having recovered her precious love
letter, was sitting down at her desk again.

"Bring it to me, please, Linda."

She knew him too well to pretend or argue. Casting a
glance of pure hatred at Elaine, she walked up to the front
of the room.

"Thank you." Mr. Russell took the paper and, without
looking at it, tore it into tiny pieces. "Now you can throw
these in the trash," he said to Linda. "I expect better
behavior from you. I'm disappointed."

Linda's face was flushed when she walked back to her
desk, and her look said clearly to Elaine, "That was all
your fault!"

Stupid jerk, Elaine thought. Imagine writing all that

junk to boys in the first place. And who threw the airplane? How come he didn't get told off? I bet it was Andrew Hayford. She twisted around in her desk to look at him, but he was bending over his desk, apparently engrossed in his work.

"Elaine!" Mr. Russell said right in her ear, making her jump. "Here's a textbook for you. I want you to work from this page. Let me know if you need any help."

Andrew had been working studiously at his math problems, but after completing four of them at top speed he suddenly felt totally unable to do any more. I have to take a break, he thought to himself. Any more math and my brain will be crushed beyond repair. He took a piece of scrap paper and wrote on it, "Want to bet you can't work out Space Demons?" Then he passed it across to Ben. Ben put up a thumb, meaning "You're on," and wrote, "A dollar?" on the back of Andrew's note. Andrew shook his head and held up two fingers. Ben smiled, nodded, and returned to his work.

I think he actually enjoys math, Andrew thought. Ben didn't appear to be bored at all; he didn't seem to need to rest his brain by staring around the room, doodling on pieces of paper, or surreptitiously kicking the person in front.

"Have you finished, Andrew?" Mr. Russell's voice interrupted him.

"I've done four," Andrew said, giving him a devastating smile out of habit. It was wasted on Mr. Russell, though.

"You're capable of more than that," he said. "You should have finished by now. Don't sit there dreaming, get on with it."

A few minutes later Ben put up his hand. "I've finished, Mr. Russell."

"Well done."

There was something about the way the teacher said it that annoyed Andrew. Ben was getting a little too smart at math these days, and Mr. Russell liked it a little too much. Andrew was not used to people liking Ben more than they liked him: It had always been the other way around. In fact in all sorts of little ways Andrew had noticed that Ben was harder to get along with lately. He was more argumentative and less agreeable, less willing to follow Andrew blindly and more inclined to go his own way. He had suddenly started having interests that Andrew didn't share, like gymnastics and dancing, and he was good at things that Andrew hadn't realized he was good at, like math. It was annoying and unsettling.

Andrew sighed and looked at the next problem. "Judy saves 41.5 percent of her allowance every week. She wants to buy a dress costing $29.99. It takes her six weeks and four days to save enough money. What does she get for her allowance each week?" He read it through again. It still didn't make any sense. He sighed exaggeratedly and rolled his eyes up at the ceiling. Who cares! he thought to himself.

When Elaine came out of the classroom after school, she immediately caught sight of her father across the school-yard. His red hair was glowing in the dullish afternoon light and he was gesturing forcefully with his hands as he talked to one of the mothers. Elaine approached him rather warily and stood at a safe distance. Sometimes he caught her up in the air like a little kid and put her up on his shoulders, which was okay—really nice in a way, if no one else was looking—but embarrassing if they were. And she was sure they were.

It was hard *not* to look at her father when you first saw him. Later on people learned to look away to avoid becoming involved in his enthusiasms, which were many and bizarre. Right now he was talking about trees, his latest obsession, and even from a distance she could see the woman's eyes starting to glaze over.

Dear Mom, she wrote in her mind, *Was it Dad you couldn't stand, or was it me?*

Her father's amber eyes were flashing as he talked. "Do you know how many of the world's trees we've cut down in this century?"

"Hi, Dad," Elaine said. The woman took the opportunity to make a quick escape.

"Hi, Elly!" For a moment she thought he was going to pick her up, but he just held her by the shoulders and, bending down, looked her straight in the face. "How'd it go?" Now all his enthusiasm and attention were on her. It was impossible not to respond—if she had been younger she would have thrown her arms around his neck.

"Oh, not bad," she said.

"Not bad or not good?"

"Really, not bad. Quite good in fact. I've got to get a uniform, though."

"It's not worth getting a uniform," he said, straightening up. "We may not be staying here long."

She'd heard that excuse many times before. Her father had a thing about uniforms. He saw them as a symbol of submission to authority, a denial of the freedom of the individual. He also disliked going shopping, and he didn't like spending money on new clothes. After all, Elaine thought, as she had often thought before, it's your mom who usually does those things for you.

"I'll get into trouble if I don't have one, Dad. The teacher said to ask at the office. Maybe they'll have a secondhand one."

His face was withdrawn now as he considered all the implications of the idea.

For heaven's sake, she thought impatiently, it's not a major decision! All you need to say is "Yes!"

"Let's just go and ask," she suggested.

"Okay," he said. "Come on."

There were still quite a few students playing in the schoolyard and kicking soccer balls around on the grass. Elaine stopped outside her classroom and looked around, disoriented. "I can't remember how to get there," she said.

"Ask one of the kids," her father said, and almost at once he shouted across the grass to the boys playing soccer, "Hey! Which way's the office?"

John Ferrone had been jumping up and down shouting, "Here! Here! To me!" for ten minutes, and nobody had kicked a ball to him. He was perfectly happy to go and do something useful instead. He ran across to Elaine and her father. "I'll show you," he said. On the way he talked nonstop to her father, his brown eyes positively melting with friendliness and sincerity. By the time they got to the office they were on the best of terms.

"Come over sometime," her father was saying. "Do you like working with wood? I'll give you a hand if there's something you want to make."

Don't encourage him, Dad, Elaine thought savagely.

"Gee, thanks, Mr. Taylor," John said. "And do you know any magic tricks from when you were in the circus? Do you think you could teach me some of those?"

"I know a few," he replied. "And don't bother with this 'Mr. Taylor' business. David's the name."

"Dad," Elaine said desperately, "if we don't hurry there'll be no one there."

"See you later, Johnno," her father said. "Hang around if you like, and we'll drive you home."

"I've got my bike."

"Put it in the back of the truck," her father told him. He saw Elaine's face. "Anything wrong, Elaine?"

She didn't answer—she could never explain her feelings to him—but as they walked into the office, she was boiling with irritation and frustration.

The secretary, Mrs. Fields, a mild, middle-aged woman normally capable of handling any crisis, was talking on the phone. She sounded very much like Elaine felt.

"How can I get hold of a janitor at such short notice?" she was saying. "It's really very inconvenient. No, I know it's not your fault, but still . . . Well, I'll see what I can do. Good-bye."

She put the phone down with an exasperated bang and looked at Elaine and her father.

"I ask you!" she said. "What am I supposed to do?"

"What's the problem?" Elaine's father asked.

"The man who cleans the school fell off a ladder this morning and broke his arm. His wife just phoned to say he'll be out of work for a couple of months. And someone's supposed to clean the washrooms every day. I don't know who I'm going to ask at this late stage."

"You could try asking me," said Elaine's father. "I wouldn't say no. I've worked as a janitor before. I've even got a couple of references if you want them."

Mrs. Fields stared at him as if he had dropped from heaven. "Could you start right away?" she asked.

"No problem," he told her. "We just have to sort out the question of a school uniform first. Can you find one for Elaine?"

Mrs. Fields gave her an appraising look. "I think we just might have something that'll fit her." She went out to look in the secondhand cupboard.

David Taylor winked at his daughter. "Getting it all together, aren't we?" he said.

He was getting it all together a little too fast for her. She could never understand how he could deliberate for ages over a small problem like whether or not to get a school uniform, and yet act so impulsively over the major choices of life like jobs and friends. Hold on, she wanted to say. I'm going to be affected by this, I'm involved. Don't I get to have a say in it? What about the famous freedom of the individual? A familiar feeling of helplessness came over her. In the middle of the office with its notices and timetables, copying machines, typewriters, and empty coffee cups, all mixed up with the smell of floor polish and the shouts of children outside, she felt herself reduced to despair. Her father was so powerful, so stubborn, so much larger than life. Once again he was bulldozing her into a place where she did not want to be.

She typed rapidly in her head, imagining darting fingers on the keys of the office typewriter: *Dear Madam, On behalf of your daughter, Elaine Jennifer Taylor, I am writing to you urgently:* HELP!

Mrs. Fields came in with a sweater and skirt. "We're in luck," she said cheerfully. "Mrs. Schulz dropped these off this morning. They're in very good shape, and they should fit you, Elaine." Holding them up against her she said, "Perfect!"

"We'll take them," Elaine's father said. "There you go, Elly. You happy now?" Without waiting for her to answer he said to Mrs. Fields, "Show me where the cleaning gear is and I'll get that little job done for you."

When they went outside, John was still waiting. "We'll be a while," Elaine's father said. "I've got some cleaning up to do."

"I don't mind waiting, David," John assured him. "I've got nothing much else to do."

"Don't you have to go home?" Elaine said.

"Nah. There's nobody there. Mom won't be home till nine—she's working the late shift this week."

Her father followed Mrs. Fields to the janitor's room.

"What do you want to do?" John asked Elaine.

Disappear, she thought to herself. Dematerialize. Become someone else, somewhere else, a thousand miles away. Aloud she said, "I dunno."

"Do you want to go on the jungle gym? You could show me some tricks," he said hopefully.

"Okay," she agreed.

As they crossed the yard, there was a shriek of brakes and rubber, and a bicycle skidded to a stop beside them.

"Hi, Mario," said John. "This is my brother," he said to Elaine.

Dark, expressionless eyes flickered over her, but otherwise the older boy ignored her. "Where've you been?" he said to John. His voice was impatient and angry. "I've been waiting for you up the street. Come on, I want to go over to the library."

"I'm going back with Elaine and her dad," John said. "He's going to show me some magic tricks."

"Magic tricks!" Mario said scornfully. His face was white and thin, and his thick black hair flopped over his forehead, hiding his eyes. His body was thin, too, and he held his shoulders rigid, as though he were constantly warding off blows. "Come on," he said again. "I'm going to play Maniac One at four o'clock on the library terminal, and I need you to play against."

"I'll see you later," John said to Elaine. "Wait while I get my bike, Mars."

Mario was already taking off. "I'll meet you up there," he shouted. He skidded through the school gate and jumped off the curb, shouting "Get out of the way!" to two third-grade girls who were talking on the corner.

Elaine walked toward the monkey bars. I might as well have a workout, she thought. It's something to do. Although she was relieved to be delivered from hours of John's company, at the same time she couldn't help feeling sorry for him. She recognized a bulldozing job when she saw one, and it was quite obvious that Mario was an expert in the field. Why are people so bossy? she wondered. Why don't they just leave other people alone? I'd never do any fighting if they'd only leave me alone to be me, but I'm always having to stand up for myself, otherwise they would just take me over.

The unwelcome idea came to her that John Ferrone's over-friendliness and her own tendency to show off were both the same sort of defense, a reaction against being bulldozed by their next of kin. The last thing she wanted was to be put in the same category as John, so she filed the idea firmly away in a compartment of her mind marked "Closed."

It was beginning to rain; the bars were damp and slippery and no good for exercising. Elaine stood by the wooden logs that surrounded the jungle gym and wondered what to do. Suddenly she felt exhausted. The day seemed to have been going on forever. On the other side of the street from the school, lights were going on in houses, making them look warm and welcoming. She wished she could walk up to one of them and slip into the life inside it for a few hours, be one of a family, have cocoa made for her, and watch television, nice and cozy.

"Haven't you got a home to go to?" Linda Schulz said in her ear.

She may have meant it as a joke, but it was so close to what Elaine had been thinking that she took it the wrong way.

"Mind your own business!" she said nastily.

"Sorry!" said Linda. "Don't be so touchy! I only meant, what are you still doing here?"

"What are *you* doing?" Elaine retorted. She felt shy about saying that her father was doing the cleaning. She was sure it was not the sort of thing Linda's father would do.

"Piano lesson." Linda swung the music bag she was carrying. "I'm just taking a shortcut home. My recital's next week." She made a face to show that she was terrified, but Elaine could tell she wasn't at all.

They heard someone whistling, and the clink of a bucket, and turned to watch Elaine's father cross the yard with a bucket in one hand and a mop in the other. He waved the hand that was holding the mop and shouted, "Won't be long, Elly. I'm nearly through."

Linda raised her eyebrows in a way Elaine didn't quite like. "Is that your dad?" she said curiously. "He's *big*, isn't he? Wow!" and she laughed.

"What's so funny?" Elaine asked suspiciously.

"Nothing," replied Linda, but she was still laughing. "I

have to run, Mom'll start worrying about me. See you
tomorrow."

She walked away quickly across the schoolyard. Elaine
started to walk back to the office through the drizzle.

Dear Mom, Are you worrying about me? Are you?

Andrew switched on the computer and the deep blue of
Space Demons filled the screen. "Go on," he said to Ben.
"It's all yours!"

Ben whistled. "Wild!" He sat down and took the joystick.
"No clues?"

Andrew shook his head and grinned. "No clues."

After a few minutes Ben said, "I don't get it. What are
you supposed to do?"

"Do you give up?"

"No way! Just give me a hint!"

"We'll have to call off the bet if I give you a hint," said
Andrew.

"Wait a minute! I just thought of something. Let me try
it." Just as Andrew had done the previous night, Ben took
off his watch and put it in front of him, the seconds
flashing.

"You got it," said Andrew, a little put out.

"Yeah? How many seconds?"

"Find out for yourself! Did you just guess or have you
played something like this before?"

"Darren programmed a game with a time control once," Ben said, concentrating on firing the rocket boosters. "But I'd have guessed anyway—there's nothing else it could be."

And I figured I was so smart! Andrew thought to himself.

"All right!" Ben exclaimed as the second screen came up. "Talk about purple rain!" The silver module collided with an amethyst asteroid and exploded. "Tricky!" he said.

"They follow a pattern," Andrew explained. "It's not hard once you know it. Let me try it, I'll show you."

"Did I win the bet or not?" Ben got up and they changed places.

"You haven't won it yet," Andrew said. "There's a lot more to come."

Ben really had won what Andrew had originally intended the bet to be, but he didn't feel like admitting that at the moment. It seemed to have been won too easily. He didn't feel like handing over the two dollars either. After all, he said to himself, Mom did say I had to make that five dollars last.

He took over the module, guiding it deftly among the flashing asteroids, twisting, turning, evading. His eyes and his hands responded instantly. His mind was on automatic. Nothing existed anymore, nothing mattered, except to keep the module going, to maintain it undestroyed, and to keep the score going up, up, up.

"Fantastic," Ben breathed beside him. "You're really good!"

The praise made Andrew feel amiable toward him again. "Watch the score," he said. "See what happens."

The score reached 9,876: The screen winked three times, and Ben drew in his breath sharply as he, too, felt with a shock the intelligence behind the game. And right after the flash of intelligence came the hordes of space demons. The sight sent a shiver through him. Andrew was playing now with fierce concentration, but the onslaught was too overwhelming. The module disappeared with a shriek, and the deep blue screen returned.

Andrew turned toward Ben and sighed. He screwed up his eyes and shook his head as though to clear his vision. "Weird," he said. "I almost felt like I was right in it. You know, not just sitting here playing it, but playing it from the inside."

Ben had picked up the box. "There's still some more stages," he said.

"Since when can you read Japanese?" Andrew said.

"I can read pictures," Ben retorted. "And I can see two things we haven't got yet—the spaceman and the gun thing he's zapping the demons with. Did you ever get to them?"

"Not yet," Andrew admitted.

"I wonder if they're related to the time factor or the score," Ben said. "What's the highest score you've ever had?"

The screen showed 19,000. "That's the best I've done," Andrew said.

"And how long did that take you?"

"I don't know, just a few minutes."

Ben had an idea. "Have you got a calculator?"

Andrew tapped his watch. "Right here."

"What's two times 9,876?"

Andrew frowned, worked it out, and said, "19,752."

"I bet that's the next changeover score," Ben said excitedly. "Whoever programmed this game was into numbers. Try again, try and beat your last score. I'll time you, too, just to check it, but I've got a hunch the time thing is a dead end."

Once again Andrew became absorbed by the game. He felt as if his whole being was connected to it. He was tireless and invincible: He could play forever. He knew exactly how and when to move, first through the asteroids, then through the space demons, without consciously thinking about what he was doing.

As he played, the game speeded up, almost as though it was trying to stop him from discovering its secrets. It became harder, less predictable; demons appeared in unexpected places. He had to think on the spot, make split-second decisions. The score was mounting: 16,000, 17,000. He was nearly there. He was hardly conscious of Ben beside him, but when 19,752 came up on the screen, Andrew heard him give a yelp of excitement. The space demons were immobilized, the module disappeared, and a spaceman in a white suit and white helmet appeared on the screen.

"He's waving at us," Ben said incredulously.

Across the bottom of the screen ran the letters ACEACEACEACEACE.

"That's me!" Andrew said exultantly. "Andrew Hayford, ace computer-game player!"

"Get the gun!" Ben shouted. It was there, black and sinister, flashing in the top right-hand corner of the screen. In the bottom right-hand corner the number 3 appeared. Andrew maneuvered the joystick, the spaceman responded, and immediately the space demons came to life again. Before the spaceman had a chance to reach his weapon, he was annihilated by a fiery orange blast.

Andrew was devastated. He felt as though he himself had been destroyed. But the screen remained the same, and another tiny spaceman was waving to them from its

center. The 3 in the bottom right-hand corner was replaced
by a 2.

"Oh, great," Ben said. "You've got two more lives. Try
and get the gun this time."

Andrew felt inside himself the vulnerability of the little
white figure, so heavily outnumbered by opposing forces,
able only to avoid them, yet needing to go through them
to reach the gun. He wasn't just moving the spaceman
with the joystick, he was reaching out to him with his whole
being, willing him to survive, to win. And when he saw
that he was going to make it, that the space demons were
outwitted and that the gun was within his grasp, he felt
an overwhelming surge of excitement.

"You did it!" Ben shouted. "Way to go!"

With the weapon in his hand, the spaceman changed.
Now he was the attacker. The game began to pulse with
an insistent high-pitched throb like a heartbeat as he
destroyed the space demons with quick flashes of red fire.
They dissolved and disappeared with menacing moans,
but there were always more of them, and they seemed to
be changing too. They were getting more cunning. They
hid, pretended to run away, and then turned to attack.
Finally two of them appeared at once on either side of the
spaceman and he could not escape. The game gave a
heavy electronic sigh. It was just how Andrew felt.

The last of the three spacemen was waving from the
screen.

"Let me take a shot," begged Ben. "I'll have to go in a
minute. You can play any time."

Andrew hesitated. He could hardly bear to stop playing.
At that moment his mother called up the stairs, "Ben,
your mother just phoned to say you're to go home now."

I can offer to let him play now, Andrew thought. He'll have to say no.

But Ben did not say no. He could not resist having another try at Space Demons. Andrew got up grudgingly and the boys changed places. Ben moved the joystick to guide the spaceman to the gun.

He got it quickly. He had been watching Andrew closely and memorizing the sequence of the space demons' attack. It was ordered, not random, and it was possible to predict what they were going to do. He was used to computer and video games, he had an inbuilt feel for them, and his hand-eye coordination was excellent. So he avoided the space demons and destroyed them, and kept the little spaceman alive longer and longer, and the score went up and up and up: 30,000; 35,000; 39,000.

"Ben!" Mrs. Hayford called again. "You must go!"

And Ben went. One moment he was sitting in front of the computer screen, totally absorbed in the game; the next he had vanished. Andrew jumped to his feet with a cry of surprise. On the screen the spaceman continued to zap the space demons, twisting, turning, and firing, but the chair where Ben had sat was empty, and the joystick did not move.

It only lasted for a moment. The spaceman was shot from behind. The computer gave a sigh, and Ben gave a gasp. He was sitting in the chair again.

Andrew stared at him, not knowing what to say. Ben's face was white, and he was flexing his right hand as though he had been holding something in it. He turned to look at Andrew, and his eyes were dark and wide and amazed.

"That was horrible," he said. "I felt as if I was right in the game, as if I *was* the spaceman, blasting the demons, and then . . . then I got blasted. . . ." His voice trailed off. He couldn't put into words the terrifying feeling of black and instantaneous nothingness that came between being shot and finding himself in the chair again. He shivered and then, pulling himself together, forced himself to grin at Andrew. "Some game!" he said. "I think I'd better go."

"No, wait!" Andrew said urgently. "What happened? What did you do? Do you think it was the score or the time?" He was immensely excited, full of questions, half-envious.

"Uh, I'll see you tomorrow," Ben said, not looking at him, sounding too offhand and too normal. He picked up his jacket and knapsack from where he had left them on Andrew's bed and made rapidly for the door.

Andrew intercepted him. "What did you *do*?" he repeated, more insistently this time, leaning against the door so that Ben could not reach the knob.

"Nothing," Ben said. "I didn't do anything! Andrew, I've got to go home. Get out of the way!"

Andrew was not going to move, but at that moment his mother tried to open the door from the other side. "Andrew!" she called. "What are you doing in there?"

He moved away, the door opened suddenly, and she came in with a rush. "Ben, you really must go at once," she said. "Your mother phoned ages ago. It's getting dark and it's raining—she'll be worried. Do you think I should drive you home?"

"No, I'll be fine. Thanks, Mrs. Hayford. 'Bye, see you, Andrew."

Ben ran down the stairs quickly, let himself out through the front door, and began to run home through the rain. It was cold and fresh on his face, but it couldn't remove the sinister feeling the game had given him. He kept thinking he could see something out of the corner of his eye. Shadows behind trees in the darkening street looked like space demons. He ran faster. He wanted to be home.

"Switch the computer off now," Mrs. Hayford said to Andrew. "Dinner's ready."

"Is Dad home?" he asked as he followed her down the stairs.

"No, he phoned to say he's been held up at the hospital."

She took a dish out of the oven and put it on the table in the family room. "Turn the TV on, would you, Andrew? I want to watch the news."

He watched the TV without taking in a word and ate without tasting the food. His mind was full of Space Demons. It was a game like no other game he had ever seen, a game that you actually became part of. It was a prototype, Dad had said. That meant no one else had one. It was unique. And he, Andrew Hayford, had it upstairs in his bedroom, and in a few minutes he was going to go and play it again.

He'd heard of biofeedback games—Space Demons must be based on the same principle. Something Ben had done had taken it on to the next stage. Ben had reached a higher score, and the game had responded. It had taken him into another dimension, where he and the electronic images had been on the same plane. And Ben being the way he is, Andrew thought with contempt, he was frightened. Ben didn't want to do it again. But he, Andrew, wasn't frightened, not at all. He was much braver than Ben. He couldn't wait!

He became aware that his mother was saying something. "What?" he said.

"Not 'what,' Andrew. 'Excuse me.' "

"Okay, excuse me," he said. " 'What' is much quicker though!"

"I just asked if you wanted any more," his mother said.

"No. No thanks."

"Didn't you like it?"

"What was it?" He had completely forgotten.

"Chicken cacciatore," she said, a little annoyed.

"Oh, yeah, it was great, but I'm not hungry."

His mother was not hungry either. She had hardly touched her food, and now she pushed her plate away and lit a cigarette.

"Mom!" Andrew reproved her. "Dad'll go insane!"

"Dad's not here, is he?" she replied curtly. She began to clear away the plates, keeping her eyes on the TV. "Do you want some dessert?"

"I'll have some when Dad gets home."

"All right. I just hope you don't have to wait too long!"

Through his preoccupation with Space Demons, it dawned on him that something was worrying her. "What's the matter?" he asked.

"Nothing." His mother gave him a smile as if to say, "There is something, but it's nothing to do with you, and it's not your fault." She put a hand on his shoulder. "I'm just tired. Put the dishes in the dishwasher for me, will you, please?"

Andrew rinsed the plates in the sink and stacked them in the dishwasher. He wondered if he should hang around downstairs and try to cheer his mother up, but he didn't like the smell of smoke, and she made him uneasy when she was in this sharp, tense mood. So he went quietly back to his room, shut the door, and began to play Space Demons again.

He had switched off the computer before going down to dinner, and when he switched it on again, the original screen appeared. I have to remember to leave it on, he thought. That way I won't need to keep playing through the early stages all the time. He took off his watch and put it in front of him. He had been planning to time the first operation, but seeing the tiny figures of the calculator on his watch reminded him of the way the program had reacted to the doubling of the score. He worked out the sum again: Two times 9,876 was 19,752, and two times 19,752 was 39,504. Ben's score had been just over 39,000 when he had disappeared. Andrew wondered if it was a question of just reaching the score, or if there was a time factor involved too. It would be hard to know for certain, if he was playing on his own.

I have to get Ben back to play it again, he thought. In the meantime I'll see what happens.

Full of excitement and anticipation, he began to play the first sequence, releasing the rocket boosters at exactly the right second. As they fell away, he was ready for the asteroid bombardment. The module responded to his deft fingers; his brain and his hands seemed to have become one. Then came the dark shapes and white faces of the space demons, implacable and menacing, but he was too swift for them. They could not touch the module he controlled. Next came the spaceman, and finally, as the magic number flashed up, the gun appeared on the screen. Andrew was impatient to get on to the next vital score, to find out for himself exactly what happened, but he had to control his impatience as skillfully as he controlled the game. He made himself concentrate purely on the task of getting the gun so that he could start to destroy the demons.

Twice he failed. The demons got past his defenses, and he felt their gloating triumph as the spacemen were annihilated. His heart lurched and his breath caught in his throat. A very small part of him was calling out in panic, *Don't go on! Stop before it's too late!*, but he refused to listen to it. Nothing was going to keep him from going on with the game, at least as far as Ben had gotten, if not farther—as far as the game went. He would not turn back or give up. He would master it or else!

With the third spaceman he concentrated harder than ever. He seemed hardly to exist as Andrew Hayford anymore. He was no longer aware of anything but the screen and the controls, the spaceman and the demons.

Then suddenly it happened. The right score and the time factor coincided at the precise point. He was no longer controlling the spaceman with the joystick. What he was holding in his hand was the gun. He had done it! He was in the game!

He was a pulsating mass of impulses and reflexes, triggered to respond to the slightest stimulus. A sudden movement, an intimation of light, caused him to swing in that direction and let his pent-up energy escape in short bursts toward the source of danger, through his hand, through the gun, and into the demons.

Razor-sharp and laser-clear, his mind had become an integrated part of his whole self. He thought with his whole body, yet his body no longer felt like a thing of flesh and blood and bone, but something more subtle and invulnerable. Mind and body worked together in exquisite harmony. His emotions were no longer conflicting or ambiguous, but clear-cut and strong: He felt excitement in pursuit and pleasure in destruction, but a controlled excitement and a cold pleasure. And when demon after demon exploded around him, filling the darkness with their moans, he laughed, but the laughter was fierce and cold, too, and came from a place deep inside him he had never known existed.

Something else—a voice—came from that place too. At first he was not sure if it was his own thoughts, or if he could really hear it. *Welcome*, said the remote voice. It had a tone of respect, almost awe, that Andrew found pleasantly flattering. *You are a champion. It is good for my children to have someone worthy to contend with. You are an ace. You will master all!*

The words made him laugh in the same fierce, cold way. You're not wrong! he said in his mind. I'm going to master this game—and you, too, whoever or whatever you are.

I am the voice of the program, it said. *You can trust me. Don't be frightened.*

I'm not frightened, he thought back, and as the gun flashed and flashed, he laughed and laughed.

But his laughter changed to a cry of horror as, too late, he saw a demon get through his defenses and felt the agonizing shock of annihilation. Yet even the plunge into nonexistence had a kind of despairing exultation about it, as he received in his own self the destruction he had been meting out.

For a split second he thought he had been sent to some place from which there was no return, and then the everyday world came back and he was sitting again in the chair facing the screen. It had returned to deep blue, and his score flashed across the top: 65,000.

There were no words to express what he felt. He sat speechless, staring at the screen. His body was tingling and shivering, and he could feel blood and adrenaline racing through him. He was amazed, excited, and exhilarated all at the same time. He could not believe what had happened. The blue screen in front of him looked so innocent, almost as if it were saying to him, "Aha! Thought I was weak, didn't you?"

It seemed a tremendous joke. He started laughing with astonishment and release. He laughed and laughed, unable to stop. "Wow!" he kept saying to himself out loud. "Wow! This is just fantastic. Unreal!"

Then it dawned on him that he was ravenously hungry. He felt drained of energy, completely used up. I'll play again later, he thought. Right now I have to get something to eat. I'm starving. I wonder how long I was playing. I wonder if Dad's home.

His father was home. When Andrew opened the bedroom door, he could hear his voice downstairs. Andrew's mind was so full of Space Demons that he did not notice it was raised in anger, but when he opened the door into the family room, even he had to be aware that there was some kind of fight going on. His mother walked abruptly into the kitchen and turned on the dishwasher. He could not see her face, but he could see his father's. He looked tired and depressed. His lips were clamped tightly together, and he looked as if he were controlling himself with a huge effort. There was something funny about his eyes— he was blinking them a lot.

"Hello, Dad," Andrew greeted him. Under the circumstances it seemed best to act as though everything was normal.

"Oh, hi. Hi, Andrew!" his father said. He was trying to sound normal too. He tried to smile, failed dismally, gave a deep sigh, and said, "I think I'd better have a drink."

He went to the liquor cabinet and poured a large shot of whiskey into a glass. "Andrew, fill this up with ice for me, would you?"

Andrew took the glass and went into the kitchen. His mother was standing staring at the dishwasher, which was starting to wash, purring away rhythmically and efficiently. Her eyes were even worse than his father's, red and watery. Andrew felt acutely uncomfortable. He pretended not to notice that anything was wrong.

"Dad wants some ice," he said. "And can I have some dessert?"

His mother stared at him blankly, as though she was not sure who he was. Hey, he wanted to say. I'm your son, remember? And you and Dad aren't supposed to fight like that. It makes me feel awful.

Her face lightened fractionally. She remembered that he should be in bed. She said so, with a halfhearted attempt at firmness.

"I've been playing Space Demons, Mom. It's unreal." He wasn't going to tell her just how unreal it was.

"Andrew, what about your homework?" He wasn't usually too enthusiastic about that sort of question, but right now he was relieved to hear it. At least it showed that she was thinking and acting like his mother again and not like that unhappy stranger.

"I'll do it in the morning. I don't have much." He automatically put on his most reassuring voice, and added a whimsical smile—not too brilliant, given the circumstances, but gentle and sincere.

His mother was disarmed by it. She put her arms around him and rested her cheek against the top of his head for a moment. Then she held him at arm's length and looked intently in his face. "Are you all right, darling? You look a bit pale."

"I've got a headache," he said. It had suddenly hit him, a reaction to tension following exhaustion, pounding behind his temples, pounding with the same throb as the game.

"You were on the computer too long. Do you want some aspirin?"

"Okay," he said. "And something to eat. I'm starving."

"You get the ice for Dad," she said. She sounded tired too. "I'll get something for dessert. What would you like?"

"Apple pie," he said, disentangling himself. "And ice cream."

Dr. Hayford took the drink to his study, saying he had some work to catch up on. Andrew ate his dessert and followed it with half a box of cookies and two apples. He still felt hungry, but his mother sent him upstairs.

"Go to bed," she said with mock severity. "Go *directly* to bed."

"Yeah, I know, I know," he said. "Do not pass GO, do not collect two hundred dollars."

He felt better when she laughed, feeble though the joke was.

Lying in bed he put his parents' quarrel out of his mind. "Everyone fights sometimes," he said to himself. "It doesn't mean anything."

The aspirin was beginning to work, and his headache receded as sleep overtook him. The hard-edged sharpness of the person who had played Space Demons seemed far away and only half-remembered. But it was so exciting, he thought sleepily. Tomorrow I'll play again. Tomorrow I'll find out what happens next.

Just before he fell asleep he realized that his hand felt curiously empty where the gun had been. He missed it. It was as though he had lost a part of himself.

It was a few days later. A freezing wind was blowing and Ben was jumping up and down just inside the school gates to keep warm, singing the words of some new dance music. He liked moving to the beat of the words. They made him feel as if he were made of molten plastic, flowing, but tough and indestructible at the same time.

The schoolyard was full of students, but nobody took any notice of Ben until John Ferrone spotted him when he came through the gates with Elaine. He came over, singing the words too.

"Elaine knows that dance," he said to Ben. "Get her to show you."

Living next door to John, Elaine had decided, was like living next door to a reporter from *Eyewitness News*. John regarded Elaine as his own exclusive scoop, and he just couldn't keep his mouth shut about her. Everything he found out was instantly broadcast to the whole class.

She shrugged her shoulders. "He doesn't need me to show him," she said. "He already knows it."

"But you can do the whole thing," John insisted.

"Let's see," Ben said.

Elaine put her knapsack down on the asphalt and pushed up the sleeves of her sweater. "This is how I do it," she said.

They all sang the words together as she went through the routine. Ben was impressed. Elaine looked as if she had the molten plastic feeling, too, and while she was dancing, she seemed to retreat to some inner place so that she didn't giggle or look self-conscious, but just let her body go as though she trusted it.

"That's terrific," he said. "Do it again slowly so I can follow you."

"I'd better put my bike away before the bell," John stated.

Ben and Elaine did the dance three or four times, and when they stopped, they were out of breath and laughing with exhilaration. Andrew, arriving at the school, saw them with a flash of something like jealousy. He had not taken much notice of the new girl apart from making monkey faces at her now and then, just to keep her in her place; ever since Elaine had started at Kingsgate he had been obsessed with Space Demons, unable to think about anything else. For days he had been in a state of excitement about the game. Every time he anticipated playing it, his heart began to pound as if it would jump out of his throat. Night after night he played it. Sometimes he made the astonishing shift into the heart of the game, and sometimes it behaved just like an ordinary computer game, exciting and challenging, but no more than that. It frustrated and enticed him. If it had behaved consistently, it would have had less of a hold over him: It was its unpredictability that obsessed him. He was sure that both the time factor and the score were involved in triggering the extra dimension, but without someone else to time him and watch the score, he had no way to check. That was why he needed to talk to Ben about it.

"Come on," he said to Ben. "Let's go."

Obediently Ben followed Andrew. Elaine stared after them. Another bulldozing job in operation, she thought to herself. It had been fun doing the dance with Ben. She had felt relaxed and, for the first time at Kingsgate School, almost happy—until mean, conceited Andrew Hayford had to come up and spoil it. Why does Ben let himself be bossed around? she asked herself. Why does John? Why do I?

The bell rang and she began to run toward the classroom. *Dear Mom, Did you have enough of being bossed? Is that why you disappeared?*

"Everybody saw your underwear!" Linda said with a giggle.

It was recess. Elaine had been trying not to show off at school, but that morning, when she had seen some third-grade girls doing handstands and cartwheels on the grass, she hadn't been able to resist walking expertly and lightly on her hands past them.

She shrugged her shoulders. "Who cares!"

"The *boys* saw them," Linda went on.

"So what," Elaine scoffed. "I just forgot to tuck my skirt in. That's not a major crime."

Linda looked more closely at the skirt. "That's *my* skirt," she said loudly. "That's where I got paint on it in Mrs. Sawyer's class last year. And that's my sweater. You're wearing my old clothes!"

"Shut up!" Elaine hissed. "You don't have to tell everyone!" She couldn't figure out whether Linda meant to be malicious to her, or if she said things like that without thinking. Linda needled her all day long with whispers from behind, loaded glances, stifled giggles, and the occasional accidental kick, but her animosity was never open or obvious. Sometimes Elaine thought she was imagining the whole thing. It made her feel defensive and insecure.

In fact she was not imagining anything. Linda's campaign of ill-will was very real and it was sending an air of restlessness through the whole class, upsetting the equilibrium that had existed before Elaine's arrival.

Linda had very definite ideas about how girls ought to behave, and in her opinion Elaine didn't measure up to any of them. Linda loved things to be pretty, neat, and matching. She loved tiny "collectibles" and took great care of all her possessions, happily rearranging them for hours. She was the sort of person who got depressed if she didn't have something new to wear. She loved pink parkas, sweaters with lace collars, and jackets adorned with patches. In the unspoken hierarchy of the class, which no one ever talked about but everyone was aware of, Linda considered herself to be pretty much the top girl, just as she considered Andrew to be the top boy. But whereas Andrew's confidence was an integral part of his character, Linda's was less assured, since she placed her belief in herself on the things she owned, rather than on who she was. When Elaine appeared on the scene, owning practically nothing but able to do things Linda could never do in a million years, Linda took an instant and profound dislike to her, a feeling that Elaine returned wholeheartedly.

That afternoon Ben became aware of Linda's attitude for the first time. He had not paid much attention to Elaine before, apart from admiring her gymnastics from a distance. Now he found himself looking at her, remembering how she had seemed while she was dancing, and it was not long before he realized that Linda was provoking her in all sorts of subtle ways.

From where he was sitting he could see Linda's desk quite clearly. She was supposed to be copying a picture of shadow puppets into her notebook, but from time to time she added the finishing touches to another picture on a piece of scrap paper. At first glance it looked like a shadow puppet too. It had a long, witch-like nose and a mass of straggly hair. Linda was carefully coloring the hair orange. When she had finished the hair, she did some extremely neat lettering underneath the picture. Ben couldn't make out what the letters said, but when he glanced across again, Linda had slipped the picture over to Rebecca Johnson, who sat next to her. He guessed that the portrait was supposed to be of Elaine. Linda and Rebecca were both giggling silently. Rebecca leaned forward quickly and put the picture on Elaine's desk.

Ben could not see Elaine's face, but her shoulders stiffened and her head went up. With one swift movement she crumpled up the paper and put it in her pocket. Then she braced herself in her chair. For a moment it looked as if she was going to push herself backward to crush Linda behind her own desk, but at that moment Mr. Russell turned around from the blackboard, and Elaine stopped.

She doesn't let it get her down, Ben thought with something like admiration. It just makes her fighting mad.

While that was going on on one side and Mr. Russell was holding forth on the culture of Indonesia, on the other side something else was going on with Andrew. Usually the two boys were in constant communication with each other all day, through looks, groans, whispers, and notes, but during the lunch break they had had an argument about Space Demons. Whenever Andrew talked about the game—and he talked about nothing else at the moment—Ben remembered with dread the terrible feeling of ceasing to exist that he had experienced. Nothing on earth would make him go through that again. Andrew desperately wanted him to come and play the game with him, but though Ben usually did whatever Andrew wanted, this time he was not going to. He had repeated his refusal at lunchtime, and now Andrew was punishing him by ignoring him, refusing to catch his eye, and pretending there was no one sitting there at all. It was as though an invisible barrier had dropped down between them. It made Ben feel uneasy and guilty and, finally, resentful. Feeling resentful made him remember something else about Andrew and Space Demons.

"You owe me two dollars," he said to Andrew as they walked out of the classroom at the end of the afternoon.

"Oh, come on!" Andrew complained. "It wasn't worth two dollars! You got it much too easily!"

Because Ben was not feeling very friendly toward Andrew, he made an issue of it. "We made a bet," he said. "You've got to keep it. You'd make me pay up if I'd lost."

"Okay, okay," Andrew said. "I haven't got the money now though. I'll give it to you later."

Ben was angry. He knew Andrew had the money because he had seen him change a five-dollar bill at lunchtime. Andrew was looking at him, daring Ben to disbelieve him, and there was something in his expression that Ben didn't like, an arrogance that had always been there but that he was now being forced to notice. He didn't want to quarrel with Andrew—he was his best friend, wasn't he?—but the lie and the arrogance outraged him. He turned and walked away without saying another word.

Andrew frowned and bit his lip as Ben walked away. He nearly called after him, "Hey, wait, I'm sorry!", but then Linda Schulz tugged at his sleeve and it gave him an excuse not to.

"You want some gum?" she said, taking a pack from her pocket.

"Sure," he said as though he was doing her a favor.

She walked beside him as they went toward the gate. "You know that new girl, Elaine Taylor?"

"What about her?"

"Her mom ran off and left her and her dad."

Usually this sort of gossip would not have interested Andrew in the least, but Linda's words brought to mind the arguments his own parents had been having. He thought he had forgotten his anxiety about them, and was annoyed to find he hadn't. Immediately he blamed Elaine for making his unspoken fears real again.

"How do you know?" he demanded.

"John Ferrone told us." Linda was chewing hard, and her eyes gleamed.

"I'm not surprised," Andrew said. "I think she's nuts."

And I'm not, he added to himself, so it won't happen to me.

"You should see her dad," Linda said. "Talk about rough-looking! He's the original apeman."

"That figures," Andrew said. "The apeman and the chimpanzee!"

Linda laughed. "Can I walk up the street with you?" she asked hopefully as they reached the gate.

"Nah, Mom's picking me up in the car," he said. "See you!"

Linda watched him walk quickly over to where his mother was waiting in the Volvo. She was feeling delighted.

"That's the best talk I've ever had with Andrew," she told herself triumphantly. "And he even took a stick of gum from me!"

The icy wind blew dead leaves around the legs of students leaving the school in twos and threes, hurrying to get home. Only Elaine was still hanging around. Seeing her sitting on her heels outside the school door, Ben felt a sudden impulse to talk to her. Something about her looked lonely and forlorn, and some kindness in his nature could not help responding.

"You going home?" he said to her.

She shook her head. "I've got to wait for my dad. He's doing the cleaning after school, but he's not even here yet." She was fed up with it, tired and cold. "He's probably forgotten what time it is," she said unhappily. "We'll be here for ages."

No one in Ben's family ever forgot the time. He squatted down next to her, just to keep her company for a while. After a few seconds he asked, "Were you really in a circus?"

"No, John got it all wrong," she replied, wrapping her arms tightly around her chest. "It wasn't a big circus with animals. It was just a bunch of people who could do acrobatics and tumbling, play music, juggle, that sort of thing. We spent some time with them. Dad drove the truck and put the tents up, and they taught me some stuff. We went all the way up the coast, working the beaches and then the country shows."

"Wow! Must've been fun."

"Yeah, it was fun." It seemed like a distant dream now—the hours in the back of the truck between towns, the long, hot endless days and the intense, vivid nights, the smell of sea and cigarette smoke and wine, and people talking and performing and then talking again, people who treated her as an equal, took her seriously for hours on end, and then ignored her for as many hours, not caring what she did or where she was—just as if she were an adult like them, and not only ten at the time.

She didn't put it into words, but thinking about it made her eyes light up, and Ben caught from her a feeling of adventure and freedom that made him look at her with interest. She was unlike anyone else he had ever known, and he wanted to get to know her better. He had an idea.

"You want to show me some of the things you can do? If Mr. Russell's still here, we'll ask if we can use the mat in the gym."

Elaine stood up. She was shivering. "Okay," she said. "At least it'll warm us up a bit."

So this is where you disappear to!" It was a week or two later, and John Ferrone came into the gym just as Elaine was showing Ben how to do a back flip. "I've been looking for you everywhere." He sounded miserable.

Really he was like a little brother, Elaine thought as she landed on her feet and grinned at Ben. Always wanting to follow her around—unless Mario was hauling him off somewhere. Most afternoons he went with his brother to the library, where they played computer games. Usually she didn't see him until she and her father got home after the cleaning was finished. Then sometimes she would go over to his place to watch television, and sometimes John would come over to help her father. And he waited every morning to walk to school with her.

Now she noticed that John's face was bruised on the left side. His left eye was beginning to blacken, and he looked as if he'd been crying.

"What's wrong?" she asked. "Did Mario belt you?"

John nodded, biting his lip as his eyes began to fill with tears again in spite of himself.

"Don't start bawling," Elaine said hurriedly. She did not like to see people crying. She had a disturbing memory—which she managed to think about very rarely—of one of the strange, unnaturally silent days after her mother had left, when she had come upon her father crying. She clenched her teeth and forced the memory away. "Tell us what happened," she said to John.

"We got thrown out of the library. Mars said it was my fault, but it wasn't—it was his. And now he's mad at me because he can't play the games for a month."

"What made them throw you out?" Ben asked. "You must have done something pretty extreme!"

"I didn't do anything," John said. "I told you, it was all Mario's fault. First he walked in with a terrible punk haircut—"

"Should suit him perfectly," Ben interrupted, laughing. "He *is* a punk!"

"No joke, Mom'll kill him. He's had his ear pierced too. He's wearing a couple of earrings. He's gone crazy."

"They can't have thrown him out of the library for that," Elaine said.

"He looked bad enough!" John said gloomily. "But there's more. He comes swaggering in, and there's a couple of guys still playing, even though it's past four o'clock and it's our turn. So he tells them to get lost, but they want to finish their game, see, and I say, 'Fair enough,' but Mars goes berserk—starts swearing at them, turns the computer off, and takes the diskette out. Then the librarian comes up, one of the women, and tells him to calm down, and he gives her an earful, so then another librarian comes up, a man—the big guy—gives him an arm lock, frog marches him out the door, and tells him not to come back for a month."

"And you followed him out just in time to get punched, I suppose," Ben said.

"Yeah," John nodded. "Then he raced off on his bike, right in front of a truck—he'll get himself killed one day. He's angry all the time, always in a rage about something. He scares me." He looked up at them with hurt eyes. "Why does he hate me?" he asked bitterly. "He's my brother. Brothers are supposed to like each other."

Elaine made a face. "That's just in books," she said.

Ben agreed. "My brother definitely doesn't like me!"

"Mario doesn't like anyone," John went on. "And no one likes him. He hasn't got any friends. You *can't* like him—he's always mean."

"Just goes to show," Ben said, "you don't have to come from a broken home."

John looked at him blankly. Ben explained, "When Mom has kids that act up in her class, she's always finding reasons for it—like their parents just split up, or they've got a new baby in the family, or whatever. She says it's the things that happen to you that make you like you are."

John said hesitantly, "I've sometimes wondered if it's not, you know, my fault? We're eighteen months apart and people take my side all the time because I'm the youngest. And Frank, that's my brother who still lives at home, he teases Mario, he says Mom wanted him to be a girl. He calls him Maria."

"That must go over like a lead balloon," said Ben. "How come he doesn't tease you too?"

"Oh, he says Mom had given up hope by the time I came along."

Elaine could just imagine it. She knew the family well enough to have some idea of the way Mario was treated. She didn't like him either, but she felt sorry for him. He was constantly put down and abused by his older brothers and his parents, while John was indulged and babied.

No wonder he hates everyone, she thought. She felt a sudden flash of sympathy for him. She could understand him. "He hates himself," she said with certainty.

"I dunno," John said. He slumped down on the mat, looking like an inflatable toy with a slow leak. "What am I going to do?" he said.

"Better take up karate," Ben said, aiming a kick at an imaginary Mario. "Elaine'll teach you."

"Don't be crazy, I don't know any," she replied.

"I thought you knew all that stuff," he said, teasing her. "Gymnastics, dance, martial arts."

She reached out and hooked his leg from under him so he fell on his back on the mat.

"There you are," he said, laughing. "Jujitsu!"

"Can't you teach me something, Elaine?" John pleaded.

"I'll teach you a forward roll," she said. "Ben can just about do one properly now."

Now it was her turn to end up on her back on the mat. She pushed herself up into a back bend, stuck her tongue out at Ben, and wiggled her ears.

John watched them enviously. "It all looks like fun," he said. "Do you do this every day?"

"I've been coming every day," Elaine said. "Ben usually has something else to do. He leads a very full life—lots of social engagements." She said it tentatively, not sure how Ben would take it. Their friendship was still being formed. She did not want him to think that she expected anything from him, or to think that she needed his company. She didn't want to need his company. Because, she said to herself when she thought about it, I'll only go away again, and it just makes one more person to miss.

"It's not my fault," Ben was saying, self-mockingly. "I come from a family of high achievers. They're always organizing my life. It's a crime to do nothing in our house."

John looked around the gym. "It feels safe in here," he said. "Maybe I'll come and hide out here after school."

"Well, don't tell anyone else about it," Elaine said. She didn't want anyone to know about her embryonic friendship with Ben. She had enough to cope with in the classroom without having to put up with teasing about boyfriends too. And she felt sure that any teasing would kill the friendship before it even came to anything.

"You'd better keep out of Mario's way for a while," she suggested. "You can come home with us. Dad'll look after you."

"Does he know any karate?" John looked hopeful.

"He doesn't need to," Ben joked. "He just looks at people and they die of fright."

"Don't insult my dad," Elaine said. No matter what she felt about her father, he belonged to her, and no one else was allowed to criticize him. "I happen to like him."

"I like him too. I'd just hate to meet him in an alley on a dark night!" Ben said. "Like now," he added, letting out a piercing scream and collapsing on the mat as a huge figure appeared in the doorway at the far end of the gym.

"I'm all finished, Elly. You ready to go now?" her father called, his voice echoing through the gym.

"Yikes, I've got to get going," Ben said, jumping to his feet. "Look at the time! See you tomorrow, Elly, John."

He ran home fast. It was beginning to get dark and it was colder than ever. When he reached his house, he was relieved to see neither of his parents' cars in the garage. He went around to the back door and let himself in.

His older brother, Darren, was sitting at the kitchen table working with a remote-control car.

"Hi," Darren said. "Where've you been?"

"Oh, up at the school," Ben said vaguely. It was always best to be vague with Darren, who operated on the principle that information is power. "What are you doing?"

"I'm trying to fix this so it works off the video control."

"Is that possible?"

"That's what I'm going to find out."

"Where's Mom?" Ben asked.

"At a meeting. Basic Math curriculum or Meet the Principal or something like that. Supper's in the crockpot. You can help yourself."

"I'm starving," Ben said. He took a bowl and a spoon from the dishwasher and walked over to the crockpot.

"By the way," Darren said, "your friend phoned."

"Which friend?" Ben said, filling his bowl with something that smelled like goulash but was otherwise unrecognizable.

"Prince Andrew," Darren said with a snort.

Ben didn't like the way he said it. "Andrew's okay," he defended him.

"He's a creep," Darren replied shortly, as he fiddled with a tiny wire. There was silence for a few moments and then he went on, "Actually, I thought you were up at his place till he phoned."

"I haven't been going there for a while."

"Don't tell me you've finally seen the light!"

"What do you mean?" Ben asked uncomfortably.

"Well, he doesn't exactly treat you very well, does he? Or are you too dense to notice?"

When Ben didn't answer, Darren said impatiently, "Well, go and phone him right away. I want to use the modem before Mom gets back."

"What are you up to?"

Now it was Darren's turn to look uncomfortable. "Never mind," he said. "Just go and phone, and don't talk for hours."

Whatever he's doing, Ben thought, putting his bowl aside and walking through to the living room, Mom'll skin him alive when she gets the phone bill.

He lifted the receiver and dialed Andrew's number. Andrew answered immediately, as if he had been waiting by the phone.

"Hi," he said, sounding really pleased to hear Ben's voice. "Can you come over after school tomorrow? I've got something to show you."

"I can't come tomorrow, I've got basketball," Ben said. "I'll come the day after." He was feeling friendly toward Andrew because he thought Darren had been unnecessarily mean and this had aroused his loyalty.

"I've got that two dollars for you," Andrew said.

This was almost an apology, and Ben accepted it as such. "Thanks," he said. "I'll see you at school tomorrow." He put down the receiver, feeling cheerful. He was glad Andrew had made the move to restore their friendship. He had missed his company after school, and it had been strange to be at school together and hardly speak to each other.

If he had been able to see Andrew at that moment, he would have felt less lighthearted. Andrew was putting down the receiver, too—with his left hand. His right hand was cradling a small, black, cylindrical object. Andrew held it close to his face and rubbed his cheek on the dense black metal. It was the gun from Space Demons.

Ben stared at the gun in disbelief. It lay in Andrew's hand—real, tangible, mind-blowing.

"Here, feel it," Andrew said. "It feels just like it does in the game, like it really belongs to you."

Ben took it gingerly. It seemed to fit into his hand as though it grew there. He gave it back quickly. His skin was prickling and he felt very strongly that he would rather be somewhere else, doing something totally safe and predictable—watching *Bugs Bunny*, for instance.

"Isn't it great?" Andrew enthused. He had no such misgivings. He was just tremendously stimulated and challenged by the new development in the game.

"How did you get it?" Ben asked.

"It was still in my hand when I came out of the game. It must be something to do with the score again. I must have activated the next stage."

"What is the next stage?"

"There seems to be a whole new program. Look."

The screen filled with a swirling, snowy pattern that made Ben's head ache and his eyes go out of focus. After a few seconds it resolved itself into a vortex that made the screen look three-dimensional and pulled his gaze down into its center. Ben found he was peering over, looking deep down into it. Then he jerked back in surprise.

"It spoke to me!" he said incredulously.

"That's what I thought," Andrew said, his face filled with excitement. "What did it say?"

"Something about hate."

" 'Respond to hate'?"

"Yes, that's it. What does it mean?"

"That's what I want to find out," Andrew replied. He tossed the gun lightly from hand to hand, hardly able to stand still. His whole being was jumping with anticipation.

"Look," Ben said, stepping back from the computer. "I don't want to have anything to do with this. I don't like it. It gives me the creeps."

"Don't be such a wimp," Andrew said. "It's the greatest thing ever!"

"It's dangerous," Ben said. "When I played it before, it said something to me then too. It said, 'You have come at last!' It wants us for something. It's just trying to suck us in."

"It's been quite safe so far," Andrew answered carelessly. His eyes seemed to be getting brighter and brighter, and he had a look of glee on his face that alarmed Ben almost as much as the Space Demons game did.

"Come on," he went on persuasively. "You're my best friend. You're the only person who knows about the game. I haven't told anyone else about it. I need your help now. I can't do anything on my own. I've tried everything with the game and nothing happens. It must be something that needs two people. Please, Ben, please say you'll help me. I won't let anything bad happen to you."

Ben always found Andrew impossible to resist when he was being his most charming. He couldn't help himself, he just wanted to please him. Andrew knew this—after all, it was the way most people reacted to him—and he never failed to take advantage of it. Now he gave Ben a grin that seemed to say that they were accomplices and buddies. "Let's play!" he said, nodding his head, certain that Ben would comply.

But Ben shook his head. He had just heard, like an echo in his mind, someone say, "He doesn't exactly treat you very well, does he? Or are you too dense to notice?" He found himself looking at Andrew with fresh eyes. For the first time he could see through the attractive face and the charm, and he didn't like what lay behind them.

He's just trying to get me to do what he wants, Ben thought. If he really liked me, he would let me do what *I* want sometimes.

"Sorry," he said out loud. "I'll play something else with you, but if you want to play Space Demons, I'm going."

"You're a real drag, Ben!" Andrew burst out. "Do you know that? I thought I could rely on you. I thought you were my friend." He gripped the gun tightly in his hand. "What's more, you're a coward. You've been hanging around with girls too much. It's made you soft."

"What do you mean?"

"Your circus friend. What's her name, Elaine. The trained chimpanzee. Funny sort of girlfriend!"

Ben was amazed at the malice in Andrew's voice, and amazed, too, that Andrew should link him with Elaine.

"Don't be stupid, she's not my girlfriend!" he said.

"You hang around with her enough. You've got pretty weird taste," Andrew taunted.

"She's just been teaching me some gymnastics," Ben said in exasperation. He wondered how they had got into this ridiculous quarrel. And what did Andrew have against Elaine? He found himself beginning to feel furious on her behalf. There was nothing wrong with her: She was okay—in fact, he really liked her. He liked the way she moved, the way she was unlike anybody else, the way she stood up for herself. It seemed totally unfair for people like Linda, and now Andrew, to pick on her. It outraged him.

"At least she's not spoiled and stuck up like you!" he said angrily.

Andrew flushed with rage and, turning his back on Ben, walked away across the room. Immediately contrite, Ben followed him. "I'm sorry," he said, "I didn't really mean it. At least . . . I did . . . but not quite like that. I really like you, Andrew. I want to be friends, but you've got to stop wanting your own way all the time. You've got to stop being so bossy."

Andrew turned around sharply. "You want to be friends? You've got a funny way of showing it. I wouldn't be friends with you anymore, Ben Challis, if you were the last person on earth. You've turned into a real creep this term, showing off, playing up to teachers, thinking you're so smart all the time. I don't like you at all anymore. I hate you!"

Something happened. Neither of them knew what it was, but they were both immediately aware of it. Something in the state of things altered, as though the world had tilted slightly, as though reality itself had shifted.

Andrew lifted the gun. The hate surged from the pit of his stomach. The gun flashed.

Ben gave a cry of horror and raised his arms in vain to cover his face. He was whirling around, tossed by an unseen force. From the computer screen came a high-pitched scream, as if something of immense power was whirring inside it. The gun in Andrew's hand flashed again and again. He could not control it: It seemed to be stuck to his hand. He could not get rid of it.

On the screen the snowy vortex whirled and whirled. Ben was being pulled toward it. He dropped his hands from his face and stretched them out to Andrew. "Help me!" he cried. "Do something!"

"Don't panic," Andrew said. "Don't worry. It'll be all right. It's just the next stage of the game. Just go with it."

Ben opened his mouth to say something, but at that moment he was whirled around again, and the next moment he was no longer there.

The noise subsided, the gun stopped flashing. Andrew ran to the computer and peered into the screen. Deep inside the vortex he could see a small figure whirling among the snowy particles. As he watched, the vortex slowed down and flattened out. The particles grouped themselves together, and they began to form a landscape: a cliff face, steep and barren. Neither the top nor the bottom was visible, and it seemed to extend both up and down forever. Then a tiny figure came into view, plunging downward. Dark holes and ledges appeared, and what looked like rough steps crisscrossing the cliff face. The little figure grasped at one of the ledges and pulled itself onto it.

Small as it was, Andrew recognized Ben. He felt a mixture of guilt at what had happened and irritation at Ben for just sitting there, doing nothing. If I was there, he thought to himself, I'd at least do some exploring. What a turkey! I'd better get in there and help him. Then he tensed and shouted, "Look out!"

A space demon was climbing the cliff face just below where Ben was sitting. Andrew watched, transfixed. He couldn't tell whether Ben had heard him or not. Then, suddenly, Ben scrambled backward into the dark hole and disappeared. The demon climbed up the cliff and vanished at the edge of the screen. Then another one appeared at the side and began to cross the cliff face horizontally. Ben did not reappear, and as Andrew gazed, the whole landscape faded and the vortex came back on the screen again.

Andrew let out all his breath in a deep sigh. He was shaking. He knew he had to do something fast. He was worried about Ben, but at the same time he was tremendously excited by the new possibilities of the game, and he was longing to get into that strange and challenging landscape. He tried to remember exactly what had happened. The vortex had been swirling, and Ben had made him angry, and he had said something. . . . Of course . . . "Respond to hate," the computer had said, and that was what it had done. He had told Ben he hated him, and the computer had responded.

He had a moment of doubt, a moment of revulsion, but they were quickly replaced by admiration for the brilliance of the game.

Now I have to get myself in, he thought. How am I going to do that?

He tried turning the gun on himself, but his efforts at self-hatred brought no response from the computer. Andrew had always been very happy with the way he was. He liked and admired himself. He thought he was great. There was no way he could force himself to hate himself.

He gave up trying. There was a knock on the door and

his mother came in. Andrew slipped the gun quickly into his pocket.

"Where's Ben?" she asked, surprised. "Has he gone already?"

"Oh, yes . . . he's . . . he's gone," Andrew said.

"He didn't stay long. Did you have a fight?"

"No, not really. . . . Well, sort of. . . ."

"That's a shame," said his mother. "Haven't you two been getting along very well lately?"

Don't ask so many questions! Andrew begged her silently, but out loud he said, "Well, you know, it's okay. I mean, we're still friends. He's just always got lots to do."

"Yes, that's true," his mother said with a laugh. "I don't know where that family gets all their energy. It makes me tired just hearing about them. Listen, I've got to do some quick shopping. Do you want to come?"

"Oh, no thanks," he said. "I'll stay here. I'd better do my homework." A plan was beginning to form in his mind.

As soon as his mother left the house, Andrew went to the phone and dialed Ben's number. As he had hoped, Darren answered.

"Is it okay if Ben stays here overnight?" Andrew asked.

"It's just great with me," Darren replied. "Both the old folks are at meetings, and I'm supposed to be baby-sitting him. I'll tell them when they get in."

Andrew put down the receiver with a feeling of deep relief. If all went well, nobody would know that Ben had ever been missing. He would have plenty of time tomorrow to get him back. He would get someone to zap him into the game as he had zapped Ben in, and then they would get out together.

He made a halfhearted stab at his homework, ate a silent

meal with his parents, watched television with his mind miles away, and went to bed. Before he got into bed he looked into the vortex on the computer screen. He wondered, a little desperately, where Ben was and what he was doing. The thought of the tiny figure disappearing into the dark hole made him feel strangely wretched. He wasn't used to feeling like that and he didn't like it. "Don't worry," he said out loud to reassure himself as much as Ben, who probably couldn't hear him anyway. "I'm going to come and get you. I'm going to rescue you. I *am* your friend." And then, just in case Ben could hear, he added, "Good night, Ben!"

He got into bed, but while he was lying down another thought occurred to him. Suppose someone came in and turned off the computer? He couldn't imagine what that would do to Ben, but just the thought of it sent shivers running through him. He got out of bed, found a black marker, and wrote on a piece of paper: DO NOT TURN OFF!! VITAL GAME IN PROGRESS! He stuck the note to the keyboard and went back to bed. I have to remember to tell Mom in the morning, he thought.

It took him a long time to go to sleep, and when he did, his dreams were full of threats and fears and space demons.

Andrew woke late, his head heavy, his mouth dry. He was entangled in his quilt, which seemed intent on stifling him; the heat had switched itself on at six A.M. and he was much too hot. He dressed slowly, feeling strung out and exhausted and somehow unreal. In the clear gray morning light that filtered through the blinds, he found it hard to believe that the events of the day before had really happened. He was sure that if he phoned Ben's house, he would find that Ben was safe at home and had been all night, but he didn't dare try it, just in case he wasn't. He took a look at the vortex, but it had not changed. It was the same snowy, swirling pattern. Waiting for me to go into it, he thought. Well, I'll be in there soon.

He straightened the quilt with one hand, pushed his pajamas under the pillow with the other, shoved his homework into his knapsack, and walked down the stairs straight into the middle of a tremendous fight.

It seemed to be about cars. The BMW wouldn't start. His father wanted to take the Volvo. His mother had a lunch date on the other side of town, and she couldn't get there without the Volvo. But like all fights, it wasn't only about what it seemed to be about. There were all sorts of other accusations and resentments coming to the surface. Andrew ducked through the middle of it and ran into the kitchen. He felt he simply could not handle another argument between his parents: He had enough to worry about already. As he was getting himself some cereal, his mother came through the door.

"What are you doing?" she demanded. She was angry, and some of her anger escaped and washed over him.

"Getting breakfast," he answered. He did not want to look at her in case her eyes were funny again.

"For goodness' sake, Andrew, sit down at the table and eat properly."

"I haven't got time," he said.

His mother looked at the clock. "I had no idea it was so

late," she exclaimed. "And I won't be able to drive you to school. Dad's taken the Volvo. You'll have to take your bike."

"Okay," he said. "I don't mind."

"I only hope it won't be raining after school," she said, looking out of the window as though his father were to blame for the overcast sky and the biting southerly wind.

"Don't worry, Mom. Even if it's pouring, I won't get pneumonia. It's not very far."

He took a last mouthful of cereal, then drank the milk out of the bowl.

"Andrew!" his mother snapped automatically. "That's not very good manners!"

"Who cares? There's no one to see. Is my lunch ready? I have to run, I'm going to be late."

"Heavens, your father wasted so much time I haven't made it. Can you buy yourself something?"

"I'll need a couple of dollars," Andrew said.

I never paid Ben his two dollars, he thought. Suddenly he wished strongly that he had. I'll give it to him as soon as I see him, he promised himself. Then he remembered and said to his mother, "Mom, please don't turn the computer off, okay?"

She shook her head as she handed him the money. "All right! But I think you're getting a bit obsessed with that game!" She handed him his jacket. "Watch out for cars, okay?"

"Mom, I promise I won't get run over," he said solemnly. "And I promise I won't get abducted either."

"Don't joke about it," she said sharply. "It does happen, you know. You can't be too careful."

She doesn't know she's talking to an ace space demon hunter, Andrew thought with satisfaction. She doesn't know anything about what's really going on. Boy, if she did, then she'd worry!

"Sure, Mom," he said. "See you!" Dashing around to the garage, he got on his ten-speed and pedaled off.

Ten-speed or not, he was still late for school. The bell had already rung, the playground was empty, and Mr. Russell was taking the roll when he arrived.

The class was tackling another episode from the inaccurately named *Mathematics and Real Life*, with varying degrees of enthusiasm and success.

"Ah, Andrew Hayford has finally turned up," Mr. Russell said, checking off his name. "You haven't got Ben Challis in your pocket, have you?"

In a way Andrew had still been hoping that Ben would just turn up at school. Mr. Russell's question made his stomach churn with a mixture of guilt and excitement. Ben really was not there. He really was lost somewhere in the computer game.

Andrew felt himself starting to get red. Assuming a helpful and concerned tone, he said quickly, "Perhaps he's got a virus."

Mr. Russell just looked at him, then marked an A against Ben's name and said, "Go and sit down. You'll have to make an effort to catch up if you don't want to spend recess doing math problems."

Elaine was completely stumped by the problems of *Mathematics and Real Life*, and Andrew's arrival was enough of a distraction to make her look up and listen. She, too, was wondering where Ben was. The day before she had thought he might come to the gym after school, and she had been disappointed when John told her he had seen him leave the school with Andrew. Now she was even more disappointed—he would not be there that afternoon either. She stared grimly at Andrew Hayford, feeling that it was all his fault. And then all at once she realized he was lying. His face was flushed and his voice was just a bit too sincere. She was sure he was lying. But why should he lie about that?

Andrew turned to walk to his desk and caught her staring at him with a puzzled expression, her eyes screwed up and her mouth open. He deliberately made a staring face back at her, opening his eyes wide and letting his jaw drop like an idiot. A look of loathing crossed her face and she stuck out her tongue at him.

Gee, this girl really hates me, Andrew thought in surprise. And then the idea came to him in a flash. Of course! Terrific! She's just the person to help me!

Before the end of the lunch break it began to rain heavily, and students ran from all directions to get under cover. Andrew had been looking for a chance to speak to Elaine without being obvious about it. He was finding it hard, for she seemed to be deliberately avoiding him. The problem is, he thought, she probably hates me too much even to listen to me. I wonder why? I've never really done anything to her. Now, seeing her heading for the classroom, he followed her in.

Linda was drawing on the blackboard. She had quite a talent for making her drawings look like who they were intended to be. One of the figures was standing on her hands with her skirt over her head. It was unmistakably Elaine. The other, standing and watching, was unmistakably John. Underneath Linda had written in pink and purple chalk, embellished with hearts and flowers: "John Ferrone loves Elaine Taylor."

"That is just so stupid," Elaine said, grabbing an eraser and trying to rub off the words. She was really riled by them. After all, she couldn't help it if John followed her around like a puppy dog. What was she supposed to do, kick him in the teeth? She tolerated him, because she more or less had to—he lived next door to her, for heaven's sake—but she wasn't sure about him as a friend yet. She certainly didn't want that sort of crack being spread around by Linda.

"Get away," Linda said, fending her off. "You're spoiling my picture."

"Darn right I am," Elaine snapped. "I'm going to erase it before anyone else comes in here!"

Linda was laughing. "Don't you think it's good, though?" She was immensely pleased with herself. She appealed to Andrew. "Don't you think it's good, Andrew? Doesn't it look just like her?"

Andrew did something that surprised both girls. He picked up the other eraser and began to rub off the picture. "It's totally infantile," he said. "Why don't you grow up, Linda?"

Linda stopped laughing as though she'd been slapped. "It was just a joke," she said in a choked voice. "No need to get so touchy!" She flushed and her eyes filled with tears. She looked down at her chalky hands. "I'd better clean up," she said, and ran out of the room.

Elaine looked at Andrew in amazement, stunned to have received help from such an unexpected quarter. He gave her a grin, and she found herself grinning back. Perhaps she had misjudged him; perhaps he wasn't as bad as she thought. He certainly was nice-looking, and he was looking at her now as though he liked her.

As they rubbed the board clean side by side, he said to

her in a low, urgent voice that no one else could hear, "I need your help. It's about Ben. Can you come over to my house after school?"

"So he isn't sick?" she said.

"No, something's happened to him. No one else knows about it but me. I'm asking you because I know you're a friend of his."

"You're not kidding me?"

"I promise I'm not. It's absolutely on the level, I swear. You'll come, won't you?" His voice was so convincing, and the look he gave her from under his thick dark lashes was so appealing, that she found she couldn't say no.

"Okay."

"We'll have to go immediately after school. We don't have much time."

"But what's happened to him?"

"I'll explain later."

·The blackboard was clean; he had no further excuse to stand there next to her. "Don't forget, right after school," he said. He put the eraser back on the ledge and went to stare out the window at the rain. How would he ever get through the afternoon?

"Have you got a bike?" Andrew asked Elaine as they came out of the classroom. Elaine watched with satisfaction as Linda, her eyes still red, walked past them angrily, pretending not to notice them.

"I could probably borrow John's," she answered. But John had already gone to hide out in the gym, and Andrew wouldn't let her waste time looking for him.

"Just take it," he said. "He won't mind. We'll be back pretty soon."

"I hope," he added to himself as they wheeled the bicycles out of the schoolyard.

It had stopped raining, but the wind was blowing more fiercely as they cycled up the hill, and by the time they reached Andrew's house Elaine's hair had mostly escaped from its braid and was straggling over her shoulders. Andrew had not stopped to think what his mother would think of her, but he caught the look of surprise on her face when she opened the door. Oh, help, he thought, another lie. I keep having to tell them. What's happening to me?

"Mom," he said, "this is Elaine. I have to lend her some books for school. We'll be upstairs for a few minutes. Come on, Elaine."

Elaine had never seen anything as beautiful as the Hayfords' house. She walked through it in a daze, trying to take in all she could, but there was too much to see at one time. She just had an impression of polished floors and furniture, pastel colors, and flowers everywhere: everything matching, everything perfect. It's just like something out of a magazine, she thought. I can't believe anybody really lives in a place like this. And there and then she made a promise to herself: I'm going to make something of my life, I'm going to be famous. And one day I'll have a house just like this.

"You're lucky," she said, looking around Andrew's room. It had a thick white carpet, pine furniture, and a sloping ceiling with dormer windows looking out over the tree-filled garden. She looked admiringly at the matching curtains and quilt, the pictures on the walls, the expensive gadgets on the shelves, and gave a sigh of pleasure. "What a great room!"

Ignoring her remark Andrew picked up the Space Demons box. "Did Ben ever mention this to you?"

Elaine shook her head.

"It's a computer game," he went on. "A really special one. My dad got it from Japan. It lets you go right inside the game to play it. That's what happened to Ben. I . . . that is, he . . . he went in the game to play it, and now he can't get out again. I've got to go in to rescue him, and you've got to help me do it."

"Well, what do I have to do?" Elaine asked. She really hadn't taken in what he was saying. The luxurious surroundings and the beautiful house had put her into a sort of trance. It was quite unbelievable that she should be standing in this wonderful room talking to Andrew Hayford, and yet she knew she was. In her dazed state of mind she was willing to go along with anything he said.

Andrew took the gun out of his pocket. "You have to shoot me with this."

"Really shoot you?" She took it, looking puzzled. "How does it work? It doesn't have a trigger."

"You hold it in your hand, point it at me, and then you . . . you have to hate me!"

"*What?*"

"You have to hate me. That's what activates the gun. You do hate me, don't you?"

"I don't know," she said. "I thought I did, but I'm not sure now."

"Well, try," he said impatiently. "And hurry up!"

Elaine lifted the gun and pointed it at him. There was a moment's silence. Nothing happened. She lowered the gun.

"It's no good," she said. "I just don't seem to be able to hate you anymore. I keep remembering how you helped me get the board clean. It was really nice of you."

Andrew stamped his foot. "You stupid idiot! I was just doing that so I could get to talk to you. You don't think I was standing up for you, do you? You don't think I like you? You know what I really think of you? I think you're an ugly redheaded chimpanzee! I'm not surprised your mother ran out on you!"

The words hit her almost physically, making her feel sick. She would have killed him if she could. The gun flashed and flashed. The vortex screamed. She saw Andrew's face get pale as he was whirled and pulled toward the screen. It was all over in a moment. Abruptly the screaming stopped. Andrew had disappeared and Elaine was alone in the room.

Andrew fell through seemingly endless space. Around him stars swirled and burned, blazed and died away. He was not frightened—everything had happened too quickly for him to feel fear. He was not even sure that he could feel anything at all. He seemed to consist entirely of the pure physical sensation of falling, like the moment when you go over the top on a roller coaster, prolonged forever.

I hope I'm not going to crash, he found himself thinking. But it was not like a landing at all. The starry particles began to thicken and solidify as he rushed past them, and he could see the cliff face forming beside him. There was a moment when the cliff seemed to be stationary and he seemed to be falling down it, but then the cliff itself began to race downward at the same speed and he realized that he was no longer moving, and that there was no up or down.

Away on the far corner of his vision he caught a flicker of movement. Suddenly he did begin to feel afraid. He had never before faced the space demons without the gun in his hand. All at once he felt vulnerable, hunted, insignificant. He put out a hand and caught hold of the cliff. Then he saw dark holes beginning to form in it: There was one just beyond him. He found that he could pull himself along the surface of the cliff, something like walking underwater on his hands. He swam and pulled himself toward the hole and plunged into it.

Something else was pulling itself up the cliff (or was it down, or across? He was completely disoriented, he had no idea of direction anymore). It made a horrible scrabbly sort of noise as it moved, and from time to time it emitted a shrill note. It was pitched so high that Andrew was not even sure he could hear it, but it pierced his skull and set his teeth on edge. He had to get away from it. Even though the interior of the hole was completely dark he crawled down into it, feeling his way with his hands.

He could see nothing, and an invisible barrier prevented him from going in any direction but straight ahead. It was a little bit like plunging down a water slide: He had to follow the direction of the slide. It was not unpleasant at all, once he had gotten used to the feeling of being out of control and in total darkness; in fact it was rather exhilarating. Andrew found he was almost enjoying the experience, but he had two anxieties on his mind. Where was Ben? And what would happen if he ran into a space demon?

At last he thought he could see a pinpoint of light ahead of him. As he approached, it grew in size until it dazzled him. He was surfacing onto the cliff face again. He felt as though he were swimming up toward it, as though he were floating, weightless, in space. The barriers of the tunnel widened and suddenly he felt something that until now had been missing from this inhuman, electronic world. It was a feeling of warmth, and with it the sound of breathing. He recognized it at once, as if it was a familiar and well-loved tune. It was a human being.

"Ben?" he whispered. "Is that you?"

"Yes it is, you jerk!"

Andrew was hurt. He had more or less forgotten that he had put Ben in the game. "I've come to rescue you," he said. "It's kind of exciting, isn't it?" He stopped, but Ben said nothing. "Don't worry, I'm sure we'll get out— we just have to go with the program."

"Yes, I know all about the program," Ben said coldly. "I've been sitting here listening to it for hours and hours. I probably know more about it than you do. It's been sending its horrible thoughts through my head. I'm telling you, it's sick! 'Respond to hate!' Who'd dream up something like that?"

"Listen," Andrew said. "I'm sorry. I don't hate you. I was just angry with you."

"It's not much good being sorry now that we're both stuck in here," Ben said bitterly. "You've done the damage already. Do you know how that program operates? It feeds on hate. That's what gives it the energy to expand. It taps into what's going on inside you, it picks up signals from your brain. The more hate there is, the bigger and more complex it gets."

"I know," said Andrew. "Isn't it brilliant?"

Ben could hardly bring himself to look at Andrew. He felt such a mixture of revulsion and horror toward him that he wasn't sure he could cope with it. The only thing he could do was hide it under a layer of indifference. The first thing they had to do was to get out of the game. When they got out he'd let Andrew know what he thought of him. But having heard the program, he was not confident.

"How did you get here?" he asked Andrew. "And did you bring the gun with you?"

In answer Andrew held out his empty hands. "Elaine Taylor zapped me in," he said. "I suppose she's still got the gun."

"We can't get out without it," Ben said. "We can hide in the tunnels because the demons can't follow us. They can only move in two dimensions; we can move in three. But to get out of the game we have to get to the top of the cliff, and the top of the cliff doesn't come until you've shot so many demons."

"You mean we can't just climb up and reach it?"

"It isn't there yet. The cliff goes on forever until the last demon is killed, and then the cliff top appears."

"Do you know how many demons?"

"Oh, no, it isn't going to tell you something as simple as that," Ben burst out angrily. "It only tells you enough to tantalize you—never enough to really help you. So what on earth are we going to do now? Have you got any bright ideas?"

"There's only one thing we can do," Andrew said. "And that's to sit here and wait for Elaine!"

Elaine was standing in Andrew's bedroom in a state of shock. Andrew's words were echoing around inside her skull as though everything else she had ever thought or felt had been stripped away. So that was what Andrew really thought of her. That was what everyone thought of her. It was just what, deep down, she had always feared: She was ugly, she was unlovable, she had made her own mother abandon her.

Her one thought was to get out, to run for cover. She ran to the door, the gun still in her hand, but as she put her hand on the knob she heard something that threw her into even greater turmoil. Someone was coming up the stairs. She could hear the quick tap-tap of high heels: It must be Andrew's mother. What could she say to her? How could she face her? What was she doing in this luxurious house anyway? She didn't belong here. And where was Andrew? Panic-stricken, hardly knowing what she was doing, she turned the gun on herself. "Stupid, ugly kid," she said to herself. "Nobody cares anything about you. You might as well be dead."

The vortex swirled, the computer screamed, the gun flashed.

Then came the falling and the swirling, and when they stopped, Elaine saw what she craved most of all—a place to hide. She pulled herself toward the hole and floated thankfully into the darkness, hoping to be able to disappear forever.

"Here she is!" Andrew said triumphantly to Ben. "You see, there's nothing to worry about!"

Ben couldn't believe his eyes. "How did you get here?" he said to Elaine in amazement. "You've got the gun too! We're going to get out after all!"

"You can both get lost," Elaine said. "I never want to talk to either of you again. And if you think I'm going to help you get out, you're wrong. I'm going to stay in here forever!"

"There's no time to waste in fighting," Andrew said. "You can stay here if you want to; we're getting out. Just give me the gun. We can't get out without it." Elaine made no response and Andrew's impatience grew. "Give it to me!" he shouted, and he reached out and grabbed it.

As soon as he touched the smooth black cylinder of the gun, an instant copy of it slid from Elaine's hand into his. Andrew took the copy: It was as smooth and black and hard as the original, which Elaine still held. "Quick," he said to Ben. "Take the gun from Elaine. Look what's happening! We're all getting one!" His voice was thrilled, his eyes gleaming. "Now!" he said with a laugh of pure glee. "Let's go hunting!"

Ben took the gun from Elaine, felt the replica form hard and cold under his fingers, and with his free hand took Elaine's firmly. He was wondering what had happened to her, what she had had to go through to hate first Andrew and then herself enough to activate the game. He felt enormously sorry for her, but he had no idea what to say to her, and anyway there was no time to talk now. He was determined, though, that whatever happened he was not going to leave her behind to lose herself in the darkness.

He was still furious with Andrew, both on his own account and Elaine's, but now that they had a chance of escape he had to admit that there was an element of fun in the game. Plunging through the tunnels, listening at the entrances for the high-pitched shrilling that announced the approach of a demon, and slipping out quickly to blast it to pieces was tremendously exciting. At first the demons came slowly, one by one, and it was easy to shoot them off the cliff face, but then they began to speed up their attack. They came from all directions at once, faster and faster, and both boys needed to shoot at the same time in order to avoid being overrun by them. When the three retreated into the tunnels, they could never be sure that there would not be a demon waiting for them at the entrance. They had to come out with guns blazing.

There seemed to be no end to the space demons. Hordes and hordes of them followed each other over the fawn-and-silver surface of the cliff. As soon as the pattern seemed clear, it changed again. Even Andrew began to wonder if the attack would ever end, if they would ever get out of the game. The noise was terrible. The almost ultrasonic note of the demons speeded up and became more and more intense; the gunfire was shrill—*pow-pow-pow*—and whenever a demon was hit, the game gave a piercing electronic shriek as though it had been torn apart itself.

Elaine thought she was in some kind of nightmare. If Ben had not continued to grip her tightly by the hand she could have hidden in one of the dark, safe tunnels and stayed there forever. Finally, on the lip of the entrance to a hole, he let go of her to turn quickly and annihilate a demon that was threatening Andrew. Elaine looked longingly back into the darkness. It was like looking into a black screen. As she stared, words began to print themselves out on the blackness: TO TERMINATE GAME REPLACE GUN HERE: REPEAT: TO TERMINATE GAME REPLACE GUN HERE. When she turned to tell Ben, she saw a demon in the corner that neither he nor Andrew had noticed, and automatically raised her gun and fired. Ben jumped in surprise as the demon exploded almost on top of him. He turned to say, "Gee, thanks, Elaine," when all the shattering noise stopped abruptly.

In the silence they all distinctly heard the program. It said, with a flattering hint of surprise, *Very well done!* Then it added courteously, *See you again, I hope.*

There was a vague sensation under their feet as though the world were reorganizing itself. The three just had time to notice that they were on top of the cliff. They caught a brief glimpse of a deep blue sky studded with stars, and then they found themselves standing once again on the thick white carpet of Andrew's room.

10

Across the screen flashed a message: CONGRATULATIONS CHAMPION DEMON HUNTERS: SCORE 250,000. It repeated itself several times. Andrew was wild with excitement and triumph. "Look at that!" he kept saying. "We scored 250,000! Wow! I bet we could get to a million! Let's try again!"

Elaine could hardly grasp what he was talking about. Too many things had happened to her in too short a time. She stared in shock at the gun in her hand. "I shot it!" she said in amazement. "I actually shot that demon thing. I saw it and I wanted to get rid of it and *pow*! It exploded!"

"And it's a good thing you did," Ben said. "I wonder where I'd be now if it had got me."

He didn't dare think about it too much. He didn't want to think about any of it. He had a horrible feeling that it had sown some vile seed in his mind that sooner or later would blossom into a full-blown nightmare. His head was aching and he was trembling all over. Everything around him looked disturbingly three-dimensional and too real, larger than life, as though his perception had started to shrivel while he had been stuck in the game. He felt shadowy and thin. He looked quickly at his hand to make sure it was still the shape it should be.

"My gun's gone!" he said in surprise.

"So's mine," Andrew said. "They faded back into the original as we came through the screen. You'd better give it to me, Elaine."

"You can have it," she said, handing it over with a shudder. "I never want to see it again."

Andrew waved the gun over his head and grinned at them. "Wasn't that something!" he crowed. "Wasn't it exciting! Isn't it just the greatest game ever!"

It was just as well Elaine had handed over the gun, because now she lost her temper with him completely. "You slime!" she yelled. "You total jerk! You conceited creep! How dare you do that sort of thing to people? You know what you said to me? You take it back!"

Andrew shrugged his shoulders, a little uncomfortably. "Aw, come on! I didn't really mean anything. I just had to make you mad at me, so I could get in and rescue Ben. Anyway, you were great. You're a champion demon hunter!"

If anything, this made her angrier still. "And what about Ben?" she shouted. "He didn't want to sit in that dumb game for a night and a day, just so you could have fun! You're an idiot, Andrew Hayford!"

"It's okay now," Andrew said. "Everything turned out all right—it's all in the program."

"To hell with the program!" Elaine said furiously. "How did the stupid program know I was going to come in after you with the gun? You could have stayed there forever, and no one would ever have known where you were!"

The thought of it made Ben feel a little sick. "How come nobody missed me?" he said to Andrew.

"You were only there overnight," Andrew said hesitantly and looked away. "I phoned Darren and said you were spending the night here."

In a way it had not been untrue, but it now sounded much more like a lie. It made Ben feel horrible, as though he had been used in some shameful way. "The whole thing stinks!" he said angrily. "Give the game away, Andrew! Don't play it anymore!"

Andrew's eyes flickered away from him. "It's so exciting, though," he said. "It's really not dangerous. It's fun. It's more fun than anything else I've ever had. I can't give it up."

"You'll have to find someone else to play it with, then," Ben retorted. "I never want to go near it again." He shivered. He felt terrible: tired, hungry, and sort of empty inside. "I'm going home," he said.

As he went toward the door, it burst open and Andrew's mother came into the room. She was very angry. Because their minds were still full of space demons, it took them a few moments to work out what she was angry about.

"Andrew, you promised you would never do that again!"

He looked at her blankly.

"You know perfectly well what I'm talking about! You were out on the roof, weren't you?"

"No," Andrew said, shaking his head and opening his eyes very wide.

Mrs. Hayford did not let him go on. "Don't lie to me, that just makes things worse. I came into the room a moment ago and there was nobody here, and now I find you back in here again, and Ben too! I suppose you came up the trellis, Ben. I told you last time, it's very dangerous. You might fall and hurt yourself. As it is, you've probably damaged the wisteria!"

She would have said more, but the phone rang and she turned to go and answer it. She directed a last angry look over her shoulder at them and said to Ben and Elaine, "I think you'd better go home."

They all had the unpleasant feeling of being blamed for something they had not done, and yet being unable to tell what they actually had been doing. It made Ben and Elaine feel cooler than ever toward Andrew. Silently, without looking at each other, they walked down the stairs, out the side door, and around to the garage where they had left the bikes. Seeing John's bike gave Elaine another reason to be angry with Andrew.

"We've been ages," she accused him. "What am I going to say to John? He probably thinks his bike's been stolen!"

"He won't mind," Andrew assured her calmly. "I'll come with you and explain that it was an emergency."

Andrew gave Ben a ride on the crossbar of his bike, and Elaine, on John's bike, cycled along behind them. Her hair blazed in the dull evening light and her face was white and angry. She was aching all over with a hurt that she could not define, and there was a lump of misery inside her that she did not want to examine or know about—she just wanted to cut it out and throw it away. She had a horrible feeling that at any moment she would burst into tears—she who never cried and who despised people who did.

As they came down the hill toward the school, they caught sight of something that made them gasp simultaneously. A white-faced, black-haired figure came swiftly out of the gate. In the gathering dusk it looked horribly like a space demon. Andrew's hand closed instinctively over the gun in his pocket. A moment later he laughed. "It's only Mario Ferrone," he said. "There's John too—I suppose they're looking for John's bike."

Mario! thought Ben. Well I never thought I'd be relieved to see him.

Andrew had never had much to do with Mario Ferrone. Like everyone else at Kingsgate, he had kept out of Mario's way while he was at the same school and breathed a sigh of relief when he went on to high school. Now high on his triumph over Space Demons, he said with a laugh, "Well, what do you know! It's the famous Ferrone brothers! Here's your bike, John. We thought you wouldn't mind if Elaine borrowed it."

John looked puzzled, but started to say, "That's okay," when Mario shoved him aside and came right up to Andrew. "*Borrowed* it!" he said aggressively. "You took it without asking—that's not borrowing, that's *stealing!*"

"It's okay, Mars," John interrupted hurriedly. "They did ask; I just forgot, that's all."

"Shut up!" Mario said without taking his eyes off Andrew.

"Oh, come on," Ben said. "I can't take this. If you two want to slug it out, get on with it. I'm going home." He took Andrew's bike, leaned it carefully up against the school fence, and started walking down the street. He couldn't help it if he was walking out on Andrew. The last thing he wanted at the moment was to get into a fight, and he felt as if his insides would all drain into nothingness if he didn't touch base at home soon.

"I'm going to find my dad," Elaine said. "Sorry about your bike, John." She pushed it at him and went into the school. She very much wanted to see her huge, redheaded father. She wanted the comfort of his presence for a while. She felt like being looked after, and he was the only person likely to do it.

Andrew did not often fight—he usually did not need to—but he had been a demon hunter for so long now that he had aggression spilling out of him. Besides it seemed almost like destiny to meet Mario like this. He could not remember ever feeling such immediate and intense dislike for anyone, and he could feel similar waves of hostility coming from Mario. They stood and glared at each other.

"Come on, Mario," John said, not very hopefully. "I've got the bike. Let's go now."

"He stole it," Mario said, spitting out the words. "He's a thief. I don't like thieves."

"And I don't like *you*!" returned Andrew, half surprised at his own boldness. Mario's appearance, the spiky black hair and black clothes, the shaved head and white face, were meant to be threatening and tough, but Andrew was not intimidated at all. Instead he felt full of confidence and energy, and bursting for a fight with someone.

The fight, when it came, was disappointing. Rolling around on the ground was much messier and a lot more painful than hunting space demons. Mario was lighter than Andrew, being of slighter build and hardly any taller, but he had often needed to fight in his life and he had the advantage of experience. Dr. Hayford had taught Andrew some karate a few years ago, but it was not much use with Mario, who preferred a more all-out, no holds barred, hand-to-hand sort of combat, and who also liked to kick a lot.

Andrew was getting the worst of it when John, who had been jumping anxiously around them exclaiming incoherently, now shouted urgently, "Break it up, Mars, break it up! Someone's coming."

The boys separated. Mario jumped swiftly to his feet and stood with one hand in his pocket, ready to start again at a moment's notice. Andrew got up more slowly, breathing heavily, and staring at Mario with implacable hatred.

Elaine and her father were driving out of the school gates in the pickup. When her father saw the boys, he pulled up alongside them and said, as if nothing was wrong, "Just going up the street for a hamburger. Anyone want to come?"

"Yeah, I do!" John said eagerly. David Taylor opened the door and got out. He yawned and stretched his arms lazily over his head. His sleeves fell back, displaying huge muscles covered with tattoos. "Hard day," he explained to Mario and Andrew. "Don't want any more hassle." He lifted John's bike with one hand and put it in the back of the truck, but before he could touch Mario's bike the older boy said viciously, "Back off, you big hulk!" He ducked the man's big hand, managed to get a last kick on Andrew's shin, ran to his bike, and disappeared down the street.

Elaine's father looked at Andrew. "You okay?"

Andrew was wishing Mr. Taylor had not turned up when he did. It made him feel like a little kid having to be rescued, when he was really Andrew Hayford, the champion demon hunter. Moreover things definitely had not been settled with Mario.

"Yeah, I'm okay," he said sulkily. He felt like adding, "Mind your own business," but close up Elaine's father was rather daunting. Andrew couldn't help remembering that he had called him the apeman. With an effort he kept his mouth shut.

The apeman said amiably, "You want to come and get a hamburger?"

"No thanks," Andrew answered shortly. "I'd better get home."

The pickup disappeared, smoke pouring from the exhaust. Andrew felt his face carefully. His lip was swelling,

he had a cut on his cheek, and blood was coming from somewhere, probably his nose. One of his knees was throbbing and his jeans were torn on one knee and pocket as well. When he discovered the second tear, he also discovered that a catastrophic thing had happened. The gun had been in his pocket. Now it was gone.

11

The next morning Ben awoke from a hideous nightmare. He had been dreaming he was climbing up the trellis to Andrew's window. With every step he took, huge pieces of wisteria vine broke off and fell soundlessly to the ground. When he looked back, he realized that a dark *something* was climbing up after him. He pulled himself up onto the roof beneath Andrew's bedroom window and saw to his relief that Andrew was sitting inside at his desk. He knocked on the window, calling for help. Andrew turned around. IIis face was dead white, his hair black and spiky. Ben just had time to realize that Andrew had turned into a space demon, when darkness came swiftly flooding up from below and engulfed him.

He could hardly eat breakfast, and he took so long getting himself ready to go to school that his mother, at first impatient, became worried.

"Are you sick?" she asked, feeling his forehead with an experienced hand, sorting out the washing with the other,

and at the same time reading her day's preparation notes, which were propped on top of the dryer.

"I don't know," Ben replied. "I feel really weird."

"Too much time spent with Andrew instead of going to sleep," she said unsympathetically. "You don't have a temperature, and anyway you can't be ill this week. I've got parent-teacher interviews and reports. You'll feel better once you get to school."

But Ben didn't feel better. If anything, he felt worse. As he cycled to school, he kept thinking he could see something on the periphery of his vision. But whenever he turned to look at it directly, it disappeared.

He put his bike in the rack and stood for a few moments in the playground, not turning his head, but looking out of the corner of his eye at whatever it was. There *was* something there that shouldn't be there. It was like a scattering of vertical black hairline cracks imposed over earth and sky, buildings and trees. The cracks gave him the shivers. He wished they would go away.

Somebody tapped him on the shoulder and he jumped. It was Andrew. Seeing him reminded Ben of his nightmare, and he recoiled involuntarily in fright.

"It's only me," Andrew said. "Did you think I was a space demon?"

Ben looked at him warily, wondering how he could joke about it. It was definitely Andrew, despite his swollen lip and the cut on his cheek.

"Here, I've got something for you." Andrew held out two dollars.

Ben took the money slowly. He was not sure he really wanted it anymore, but he did not know how to refuse it. "Thanks," he said. "Are you okay? What happened with Mario?"

"We fought it out!" Andrew said. He sounded quite pleased about it.

"So how come you aren't in the hospital?"

"Oh, you know, Mario's not as tough as he thinks he is. But something bad did happen. I lost the gun."

"So you can't get back in the game anymore?" Ben felt a wave of relief sweep over him. It was short-lived.

"I'll get back in the game all right," Andrew said confidently. "I'm sure of that. I reckon Mario must have picked up the gun when we were fighting. I'll just have to get it back off him."

Ben sighed. Andrew seemed determined to run headlong into trouble on every front. He stared straight ahead, not knowing what to say, and not wanting to look sideways at the black cracks. On the other side of the schoolyard someone with fiery red hair walked into his field of vision. He watched with foreboding.

Elaine took a couple of paces forward and then stood still, not turning her head. He was too far away to see her eyes, but he didn't need to. He knew exactly what she was doing because it was just what he had been doing: She was looking out of the corners of her eyes at something that shouldn't be there.

During Creative Writing he sent her a note: "What are you looking at?" She sat in the row in front of him to his left and it was easy to flick the note across to her, but when she sent back her reply, Mr. Russell, in an excess of vigilance, intercepted it.

"This is from you, isn't it, Elaine?" he asked politely. "Perhaps you can tell us what it means." He read, " 'What are you looking at? Black cracks in the world.' "

"It's part of my story," Elaine said desperately. "Science fiction."

"It sounds very inventive. You can read all of it to us when you've finished. In the meantime please keep your inspiration to yourself."

"The trouble was," Elaine said at lunchtime, "I'd started writing a story about ballet dancers. It was rather hard to turn it into science fiction." She'd had to spend recess doing it.

"The cracks—can you still see them?" Ben asked.

"They're there all the time. Can you see them too?"

"Yes."

"I thought you must be able to. Creepy, aren't they? What do you think they are?"

"I don't know," he replied. "Something to do with Andrew's precious game, probably." He had been trying to ignore them, but he was always conscious of them. They made him feel uneasy and oppressed.

"I had a terrible nightmare last night," he said.

"About Andrew?"

"Yeah."

"I did too," she said, not looking at him.

"What are we going to do about it?"

"Nothing!" Elaine said crossly. "It's his own stupid fault. He shouldn't mess around with things like that. I'm not going to help him get out of it. Don't worry about him. He'll be all right."

But Ben was not so sure. He was worried—about Andrew, about the black cracks that would not go away, and about the space demons. He could not concentrate on schoolwork at all that afternoon. The day dragged past. He gazed out of the window; he felt dreamy and jumpy in turns; and when he doodled pictures on scrap paper they all turned into black lines.

Andrew was restless too. He was trying to work out the best way to approach Mario, whether to go to his house or wait for him outside the high school. There was something else bothering him, too, something he did not want to admit to himself. Something was making him very uneasy, and he was shutting his mind to it. Not only his mind, his eyes too. He had the feeling that there was something hovering behind him, just out of his line of vision. It was threatening to unleash on him a terrifying feeling of responsibility for disaster.

Everything's okay, he kept saying to himself. Nothing's gone wrong. It's just a game, it's nothing more serious than that. There isn't really anything sinister about it. I just have to trust the program. Little tentacles of dread were beginning to wind themselves around his mind, but he refused to take any notice of them. Instead he let his mind roam in that other landscape. He kept reliving the thrill of the dark tunnels and the fawn-and-silver cliff. He kept remembering the moment of absolute triumph when the cliff top had formed under their feet. He wanted to get back there. He wanted to stay longer under that starry sky and discover all its secrets. He wanted to hear the admiring voice say, "*Very* well done!"

Elaine could not sit still. She found sitting still hard enough at the best of times, but when she was disturbed about something, she felt she had to express it in physical activity or she would explode. And despite what she had said to Ben, right now she was very disturbed. She could not forget Andrew's taunting her yesterday. She kept telling herself he had not really meant the words, but, like a tongue continually seeking out a sore tooth, her mind kept returning to them. "Ugly redheaded chimpanzee. No wonder your mother ran out on you!"

Dear Mom, Why did you just disappear? Why did you wipe me out? Please answer me! I need to talk about it. I need to know.

She fidgeted and wriggled in her chair. She wiggled her ears and bent her double-jointed fingers back. And she kept turning her head sharply from side to side trying to see clearly whatever it was that she felt creeping up on her.

When the bell rang at the end of the afternoon, everyone heard a sigh of relief. Linda, jumping up quickly to get outside, caught the end of Elaine's braid and pulled it sharply and not quite accidentally. In retaliation Elaine put out her foot as Linda went past, and the blond girl tripped and nearly fell.

"Elaine," Mr. Russell said wearily. "Stay behind for a moment. I want to talk to you."

Elaine frantically signaled Ben to wait for her, and stood by the teacher's desk as the classroom emptied. Mr. Russell was stacking papers in a neat pile, ready to take them home to mark, and tidying up his desk. Elaine had to wait for several minutes. She did not wait patiently.

"Now," he said at last, looking up at her, "how are the gymnastics going?"

She had expected to be told off. This approach took her by surprise. Her face relaxed and she almost smiled at him. "It's okay," she said.

"Are you feeling at home here now?"

She nodded.

"Making friends?"

"I dunno." She shrugged her shoulders. "I suppose so."

"Then what's the problem?"

"The problem?" She looked blankly at him.

"Passing notes, fidgeting all afternoon, tripping people up—quite apart from achieving absolutely no work at all. Is there something wrong?"

"No, not really," Elaine said. Then, when Mr. Russell continued to stare at her without saying anything, she went on defensively, "Linda's always picking on me."

"And you never do anything to Linda, of course!"

"I'm only standing up for myself," she answered fiercely.

"It's a shame you two can't be friends," he said. "You'd probably find you've got quite a lot in common. I think you'd be good for each other."

"You can't be friends with someone just because it seems like a good idea," she argued.

"Can't you?" Mr. Russell put the papers in his bag and stood up. "Why don't you give it a try?" When she didn't answer, he added, "I'll come by the gym one day soon and make sure you're not breaking your necks." He smiled at her and walked quickly out of the classroom.

Elaine ran across to where Ben was waiting with John. They were both staring out the gate, a look of astonishment on their faces. On the opposite side of the road Andrew and Mario were deep in conversation. As the three of them watched, the two boys got on their bikes and began to pedal up the hill toward Andrew's house.

John let out his breath in a whistle. "What are they up to? Yesterday Mario was swearing he'd pulverize Andrew. Now they're all buddy-buddy!"

Elaine and Ben exchanged glances. They had a pretty good idea what Andrew was up to, and they didn't like it at all.

"There's nothing we can do about it," Elaine said. "Let's go to the gym. I need a really good workout to get myself straight again."

But not even an hour in the gym could erase the black cracks in the world.

12

Andrew had not needed to search for Mario. Mario had come looking for him. When Andrew was finally released from the tortures of school, Mario was waiting outside on his bike.

Andrew crossed the road toward him without hesitating, feeling instinctively that a frontal assault was the best attack. He was gratified to notice that Mario's left eye was swollen and slightly blackened.

"You've got something of mine, haven't you?" he said. He was also pleased to discover that the antipathy between them was greater than ever. Hostility oozed blackly out of Mario like an oil slick. He gave Andrew a dark look from under his brows, and said nastily, "I'm not going to give it back to you. I just want to know what it's for."

Andrew stared at him for a few moments before he answered. In some way he could not explain, he was convinced that the gun had brought them together. It was all part of the program. His quick brain had already seen the possible connection between the "Respond to Hate" program of Space Demons and someone as hostile and hate-filled as Mario. But how could he use Mario to get back into the game?

"You don't have to give it back," he said. "It's part of a game. If you come up to my place, I'll show you how to play it." He said it nonchalantly, trying to hide his eagerness.

Mario studied him briefly with narrowed eyes and then abruptly took the gun out of his pocket and weighed it in his hand. "I like it," he said in a sinister, purring voice. "It's powerful."

"Yeah," replied Andrew, keeping his voice casual and careless. "It's powerful all right. You've got no idea how powerful. But you can't use it on its own. It's got to be part of the game. Come on, I'll show you."

"What's in it for you?" Mario asked suspiciously.

"The game's no good without the gun," Andrew said. "And the gun's no good without the game. So we have to cooperate."

He was afraid he was pleading too much, but he had underestimated the power of the gun. Mario was already hooked by it. He had been carrying it around all day, taking it out and looking at it, stroking it, feeling how it fitted perfectly into his hand. Almost unconsciously he had been driven to come and find Andrew, because he had to discover how to use the gun. Now, unable to hide the burning urgency in his voice, he said, "What are we waiting for? Let's go!"

"You've got a big place," Mario said as they left their bikes in the garage. "What's your dad do?"

"He's a doctor," Andrew replied shortly. Mario looked disgusted, which made Andrew dislike him even more. They went into the house by the side door. Mario walked like a cat in a new place, alert and suspicious, eyes everywhere, ready to run.

Gosh, I'll have to keep an eye on him, Andrew thought. I hope he doesn't steal anything.

His mother called out from the living room. "Is that you, Andrew? I'm on the phone. I'll be a little while."

"I've brought someone home," he said, putting his head around the door. "We'll be upstairs. Who are you talking to?"

"Kaye," she said. Kaye was her oldest friend; the conversation would go on for ages. Andrew led Mario up the stairs.

"This is the game," Andrew said, showing him the computer. Mario looked envious. He had already cased Andrew's room with one swift glance. "How come you've got so much stuff?" he asked belligerently. "Your parents must really spoil you."

"It's a special game," Andrew continued, refusing to be angered, glad only to see that Mario was such a dedicated hater. He leaned forward and whispered, making his words sound dramatic and exciting, "If you have the gun, you can get into the game and go demon hunting!"

Mario jumped slightly, as though Andrew had touched some hidden nerve. He took the gun out of his pocket. His hand was quivering.

"How do you do it?" he whispered back.

"Listen very carefully. Don't forget anything I say. It could cost you your life." Mario's eyes widened as he hung on every word. "You'll find yourself next to a cliff. Make for the tunnels. The demons can't follow you in there. When you've killed enough of them, the program brings you to the top of the cliff, and you'll be back here again. Are you ready to do it?"

"Of course I'm ready," Mario hissed. "How do you get in?"

"The game responds to hate. If you can hate yourself, the gun will take you in."

"I have to shoot myself with this thing?" Mario looked at him incredulously. "No way, man. I don't trust you. You show me first." He almost started to hand the gun over to Andrew, but then he thought better of it. He put it up to his cheek and frowned.

"I can't show you," Andrew said. His palms were sweating slightly. I must be nervous, he thought to himself. Something's getting to me. He turned his head slightly to one side. For a second he'd thought there was something just behind him, but there was nothing there. He looked squarely at Mario. "I can't hate myself enough."

"Oh, yeah?" Mario sneered. "I'd have thought it was a cinch!"

The air between them trembled. Reality prepared to alter. Andrew found himself automatically reaching for flattery. He had to get Mario to hate himself, without hating Andrew by mistake. Otherwise I'll find myself stuck in there, he thought with a shiver. "You're a great hater," he said calmly. "One of the greatest, I can tell."

"Yeah, well, you're right about that much," Mario retorted. "There's not a single person in the whole freaking world I don't hate. I hate them all!"

"Including yourself?"

"Absolutely!"

"I don't believe you," Andrew said cunningly.

Mario's eyes gleamed and then narrowed to slits. "Watch this!" He held the gun up to his head and closed his eyes. A few moments passed in silence. The vortex swirled. Andrew blinked and turned his head from side to side. His apprehension deepened. His heart was thudding.

Nothing happened. Mario lowered the gun.

"What's the problem?" Andrew asked. His voice surprised him. It didn't sound the way it usually did.

"Shut up!" Mario said savagely. He raised the gun again, giving Andrew a nasty look. "If you're kidding me, I'll take you apart," he threatened.

He leaned right over the screen and tapped his nails on top of the monitor. He seemed to be muttering something to himself, with his shoulders hunched and his body clenched stiffly.

"What are you doing?" Andrew whispered after a few seconds.

There was no answer, but Mario's voice grew slightly louder. Andrew listened in a mixture of embarrassment, horror, and fascination.

"You freaking little punk," Mario was saying to himself. "You bloody little reject! You no-good hopeless jerk. You should have been born dead!"

He turned slowly around to face Andrew. At the sight of the twisted, hate-filled face Andrew dodged sideways, but Mario was not aiming the gun at him. He was holding it firmly against his own forehead. His eyes were open and Andrew could see in them a strange, disturbing mixture of pain and triumph. The gun flashed. The vortex screamed. Mario disappeared.

Andrew ran to the screen and peered into it. He saw the small figure spinning into the vortex, saw the cliff face form, and saw Mario make his way into the nearest tunnel. He's brave, he thought grudgingly, But can he do it? What if he doesn't make it out again?

He felt momentarily sick at the thought. He could hardly bear to watch the screen, nor could he bear to tear his gaze away from it. He watched the demons start to advance across the cliff face and watched Mario destroy his first one, then his second and his third, until Andrew lost count. He's really good, he thought with unwilling admiration. But can he handle them when they start to speed up? We only just made it, and there were three of us. There's only one of him.

It was almost unendurable. Time and again Andrew thought Mario had not seen a demon creeping up on him from behind, and time and again he turned at the last moment and destroyed it. At last the final demon exploded in a burst of orange flame, and the cliff top swung into being beneath the stars. Andrew just had time to wish passionately that he was there, too, and then Mario was standing next to him again, the gun in his hand.

Immediately words printed out across the screen: CONGRATULATIONS ACE DEMON HUNTER: SCORE 200,000.

"Pretty good," Andrew said, turning away so that Mario would not see how relieved and impressed he was.

Mario's face seemed to have come alive. His eyes were wide and blazing, and for the first time ever Andrew saw something like a smile on his lips. Even his body seemed to have relaxed. He no longer held his shoulders rigid with tension. He swung the gun lightly from hand to hand.

"Man," he said to Andrew, "that was wild! That was really something!"

"You got a good score," Andrew said casually. "It's not the top one though."

"Who got the top one?" Mario demanded. "I bet I can beat it!"

"We got 250,000 just yesterday," Andrew said. "There were three of us, but I know you and I could beat that. I reckon we could reach a million together. That's what I want to do. You zap me in, then follow me. We'll meet in there: Once we're in, we can duplicate the gun. But first you have to zap me."

"I have to hate you with the gun?"

"You catch on quickly. Exactly."

Mario laughed. It was not a pleasant sound. "Make my day!" he said. "You spoiled, rich creep!"

The wave of hatred and contempt caught Andrew in the stomach. He gasped as the vortex pulled him into the screen. He saw the gun flash again almost instantaneously and saw Mario being pulled after him. Together they fell into space. Together they plunged into the tunnel. Then Andrew drew his clone gun from Mario's, and the great demon hunt began.

As they reappeared in the room, 400,000 flashed up on the screen. Andrew was shaking and his head ached from the noise of the game. Mario's eyes were feverish in his pale face; the hand that held the gun was trembling. He turned his head quickly from side to side.

"I can still see things," he said. "Those demons are still creeping up on us."

Andrew spun around, but he could not quite see anything there. Then he thought he saw a space demon on the other side of him, but when he spun around again, it was only Mario's reflection in the mirror. Their eyes caught and they stared hard at each other.

"Fantastic game!" Mario said. "When do we play again?"

"Tomorrow," Andrew said. "I don't want my mom to know about it. She'll be up here any minute."

Mario considered this impassively. Then he nodded. "I'll meet you outside school. See you!"

He put the gun in his pocket and ran down the stairs to the front door, giving Andrew's mother a brief wave as he passed the living room. Then he let himself out and was gone. A few moments later Andrew walked downstairs. He was exhausted. The real world seemed dreamlike, and he felt strung out and shadowy. His hand felt insubstantial, as if it would go straight through the banister. I'd better get something to eat, he thought. That was about all he could think: His brain seemed to be in cold storage.

His mother was still talking on the phone. As he went past the living-room door he heard her say, "But how am I going to tell Andrew?"

Tell Andrew? Tell Andrew what? His frozen brain tried to tell him something was wrong, but it couldn't work out what or why. He went into the kitchen with the words still echoing meaninglessly inside his head. He put the kettle on, took a box of chocolate cookies out of the cupboard, made a cup of instant coffee, and ate five cookies. As he was eating his sixth, he heard the telephone receiver being put down.

"Andrew, who was that boy?" His mother came into the kitchen. She did not look happy.

"Oh, just someone I know."

"He's not at Kingsgate, is he?"

"No, he's in high school." Andrew was on his eighth cookie now. "He was at Kingsgate last year."

She took the box of cookies away from him. He knew she wanted to say something about Mario, but she didn't want to seem impolite or prejudiced.

"He looked a bit rough, darling," she ventured finally.

A bit rough! Andrew thought. That's an understatement! He cast around in the frozen wastes of his non-functioning brain for something that might reassure her.

"He's interested in computers," he said. "I said he could have a shot at ours."

Once again his mother seemed to hesitate, stuck between wanting to say something and not wanting to say the wrong thing. She changed the subject. "Are you drinking coffee? I didn't know you liked it."

"I thought it might wake me up a bit."

She studied him in silence for a few moments. Poor Mom, he thought. I'm giving her more to worry about.

Mrs. Hayford seemed about to say something several times, but then she changed her mind. "Well, I'd better start getting dinner," she said finally. "I think I've got some steak in the freezer. Would you like salad with it?"

"Okay," Andrew said. "Is Dad going to be home for dinner?"

His mother paused almost imperceptibly before answering. "He's gone to the city for a few days."

He felt awake enough to find this peculiar. The coffee was beginning to work.

"So how come he didn't say anything about it?"

"It came up very suddenly," she said. She stopped for a moment and then went on, "Andrew, you know that we both love you very much."

Somewhere in the cold, white spaces warning bells began to ring shrilly. "Well, sure," he said rather uncomfortably.

"I just want you always to remember that," she said in a voice that sounded quite unlike her own. "I want you to remember that we both love you."

Suddenly he had absolutely no desire to finish the conversation. He didn't want to think about where it was heading. It was much too dangerous. It threatened to turn him from a champion demon hunter into a vulnerable and powerless child. So he got up suddenly, said, "I'd better do my homework," and bolted out of the room.

13

The next day Andrew and Mario played Space Demons again, and the next day, and the day after that. On the third night Andrew had a nightmare. He dreamed he was opening his eyes. It was pitch dark, as dark as inside the tunnels. He tried to reach out to turn on the bedside light, but he seemed to have lost the use of his arms. He could not move at all. The darkness was so complete that he himself seemed a part of it. He could feel his heart pounding with a curious rhythmic *thud thud thud* that was not quite its own. The pulsing went through him, through the darkness that was also him, through the whole room, with a sort of silent echoing that chilled his blood and made his skin crawl. He opened his mouth to scream but no sound came. The darkness stretched away forever into eternity. The whole universe was blacked out. There was nothing out there at all, nothing except a faintly mocking *something*. He could not see or touch or hear it, but he could sense it inside him and around him. He knew that now it owned and possessed him, while his own self shriveled pathetically and died. Then the *something* spoke to him. *Bad luck!* it said. It was the voice of the program, but it had lost its suggestion of flattery, now it only mocked. *You did quite well. Yes, really quite well. I should have told you before. But no one has ever mastered my children. Now you must become one of them.*

"Andrew! Get up! You're going to be late for school!"

Andrew woke up with a cry. He sat bolt upright in bed and stared at his mother with blank, uncomprehending eyes. The pulsing through the room shrank and retracted, to become again the beating of his heart. He could move again, but barely. He felt as if he had not slept at all. His limbs were heavy and aching.

Mrs. Hayford turned from the window, where she had been raising the blinds, and looked at him with concern. "Are you feeling all right? You're not ill, are you?"

Panic made him angry. He found himself shouting at her. "Mom, will you stop treating me like a baby? Of course I'm all right. Now get out and let me get dressed."

He was not usually rude to her. He had always had beautiful manners. The blood drained from his mother's face. "There's no need to talk to me like that. You can at least be polite."

"Sorry," Andrew mumbled. "I had a really bad nightmare."

His mother came and sat down on his bed next to him and put her arm around him. "It's all right," she said. "I know things are tough right now. It's perfectly normal to feel anger and hostility toward me. Don't worry about it. I understand."

What is she talking about? Andrew thought. Does she know about the game?

"I've been worried about you, Andrew," she went on. "I spoke to your teacher last night. He said he'd noticed a change in you at school. I don't want you to be rude and aggressive, but I do understand why you feel you have to be. . . . I know that's not what you're really like. It's just a reaction to the circumstances at the moment. I told Mr. Russell that. He understands."

That's great, Andrew said to himself. Everyone understands me—the only trouble is, none of them knows what's
really going on. And how can I possibly tell them?

Pushing his mother's arm aside, he flung back the quilt
and got out of bed. "I'd better get dressed, Mom."

He studied his reflection in the mirror. When he had
first gotten out of bed, he thought his face looked paler
and his hair darker than usual. It must have been just a
trick of the light, though; now when he looked at himself
his hair looked as blond, his face as tanned, and his eyes
as blue as ever.

"The boy who was here last night," his mother began
tentatively. She made no move to go, but remained sitting
on the bed. "What's his name?"

Oh, no, Andrew thought, she's not going to start on
that again! Out loud he said, "Don't worry about him,
Mom. I can handle him."

"*Handle* him? That's a funny word to use about a friend."

"Well, he's not exactly a friend." Andrew picked up his
clothes from the chair. He wished his mother would go so
he could get changed.

"I'm not very happy about him coming here," his mother
said.

Andrew knew it was her way of saying that she did not
want him to come over anymore. Why on earth doesn't
she just say so? he thought, irritated. The sight of her
worried face was beginning to fill him with unreasoning
fury. He felt like hurting her.

"I don't think it's any of your business," he said rudely.

As if she wanted to back off from a confrontation, she
got up and walked toward the door. She looked at him
reproachfully from the doorway, her eyes suspiciously
bright. He refused to look back.

"Get dressed and I'll fix your lunch," she said in a choked sort of voice, and she disappeared quickly down the stairs.

When Andrew walked into the classroom, Mr. Russell was already teaching the first lesson. He frowned when he saw Andrew come in. He felt he should tell him off—it was the third time he'd arrived late that week—but after his conversation with Mrs. Hayford the night before, he felt perhaps he should be lenient. So all he said was, "Sit down quickly, Andrew, and get your books out. Please try to be on time tomorrow."

Funny, Andrew thought as he sat down, I thought he'd say something really heavy. He almost sounds as if he's sorry for me.

He didn't think about it anymore. He thought about Space Demons instead.

He and Mario were getting more and more skillful at the game: Their scores were getting higher and higher, and every day they disliked each other even more. Inside the game they had to work together to master it; they had to defend, sometimes save each other. But when Mario blasted a demon that was threatening Andrew, it was not really done to save him, but rather to prove that Mario was the better player, to show contempt. Andrew responded with greater and more bitter hatred, determined that the next time he would be the one to save Mario, the one to deal out the contempt instead of receiving it. Sometimes he was tempted to stand back, to do nothing and let Mario be blasted. He shivered now, thinking about it. What would happen? It would be so easy—it didn't even have to be deliberate. The game was also becoming more demanding. Every time they played it, it was harder. It would only be a matter of time before one of them made a false move or an error of judgment . . . and then what?

I don't suppose there's any *real* danger, he thought. The program will take care of everything. You probably just come out of the game, like in the other stage when the last spaceman gets shot. But somewhere in his mind there was a feeling he could not quite recall, a memory of words someone or *something* had spoken deep into his very being, a blackness he could not shake off.

"Andrew Hayford, are you with us this morning or are you somewhere else?" Mr. Russell's voice was uncharacteristically gentle and polite. Andrew opened his mouth to answer, but as he did so he caught sight of something at the window opposite him. Instead of answering equally politely, as he'd intended to, he jumped to his feet and screamed, "Go away! Get away from me!" Then he spun around to look behind him, his eyes wide, his face rigid with fear.

In three strides the teacher was beside him, gripping his shoulders. "Calm down, Andrew!"

The classroom was totally silent. Nobody moved a muscle. Everybody stared at Andrew, stunned by his outburst, eagerly waiting to see what would happen next. But Elaine, too, had been staring out of the window, and she'd seen what Andrew had seen—the reflection of a pale face with spiky black hair. And Ben, looking in the other direction over Andrew's desk, saw a flickering black figure appear and then disappear behind him.

Ben took a quick look behind his own back and saw a black line sliding away. Had he imagined it, or was it more distinct than before? He looked the other way. This time there was no doubt about it. The lines were getting thicker. They were no longer really lines anymore. They were spreading out, like a dark stain, but a stain with a definite shape, and with a splash of white up toward the top, where a face would be. . . . He jammed his hand over his mouth to stop from screaming out.

"There's no need for everyone to stop working and stare," Mr. Russell said acidly. "I want two pages finished by the end of the lesson. Andrew, come outside. I want to talk to you for a couple of minutes."

Andrew followed his teacher into the corridor. He had himself under control again now. How stupid he had been to be frightened! It was just that the reflection in the window had been so real, so menacing. But of course it could not harm him. It was just something to do with the game. He couldn't wait to find out what. He was dying with impatience to get through the day, meet up with Mario, and get back into the game again. How totally boring school was in comparison! How could anyone be expected to take it seriously?

He missed some of what Mr. Russell was saying to him. Now the teacher was looking at him with compassion. Andrew did not care for the look. He did not want to be pitied. It made him feel that there was something wrong with him. He would have preferred admiration and respect.

". . . a rough time for you," Mr. Russell was saying. "If there's anything I can do to help, just come and talk to me."

Anything you can do! Andrew thought. What could you possibly do? And how could I possibly talk to you? You wouldn't believe a word I was saying, for one thing. And even if you did believe me, you'd never be game enough to try out Space Demons. I'll bet you can't even play Pacman!

"You're probably finding it hard to concentrate at the moment," Mr. Russell was saying. "That's a perfectly normal reaction."

It is? Andrew thought. How does he know? And why is everybody so concerned about me all of a sudden?

He wondered if he could put this concern to some profitable use. He gave Mr. Russell a wan but disarming smile. "I do feel a bit strange," he said. Perhaps he would be able to get off from school for the day.

"Your mother and I agreed that it's best for you to keep to your usual routine—otherwise I'd let you go home. Go and sit down and do the best you can. And don't forget, if you feel like talking to someone, I'm always here."

Once again Andrew felt a wave of irritation at the teacher's concern. When they returned to the classroom, the way everyone looked at him made him even angrier. Why doesn't everyone mind their own business? he thought furiously. And when Ben mouthed across at him, Are you okay? he made an ugly sneering face back at him and refused to look in his direction for the rest of the day.

Inside him the fire of hate grew stronger and stronger. It was slowly consuming him.

14

Facing Mario at last in his room, Andrew was burning with resentment and rage. From the look of him, Mario felt the same. His eyes were dark and cold, his face sullen.

He drew the gun from his pocket and gripped it tightly. Then he gave a flickering, contemptuous look at Andrew.

"Ready?" he sneered.

Andrew braced himself for the gun's flash, for the wave of hatred that would take him into the game. It hit him as always with sickening force, making him bite his lip to prevent himself from gasping. The swirling vortex dragged him into the game. His heart began to hammer in time with the electronic pulse, and as he fell past the cliff face the same pulse flashed before his eyes in measured beats of black and fawn and silver. As the particles solidified and began to rush downward, and the black holes started to form and become hollow, he saw below him a flicker of movement. The demons were coming out already, before he had a chance to reach the safety of the tunnels. Terrified, he flung himself at the cliff, only to bounce back from it as if from a force field.

Take it easy, he told himself. Don't panic. Remember the first sequence.

He could see it in his mind's eye. First one demon advanced across the cliff face, then three in a row, from right to left. They were followed by four rising simultaneously from the bottom, then one again from left to right. The first blast shot past him, blazing orange. He slid a fraction upward, saw the next three coming, and flattened himself horizontally. Two shots went above him and one below. Now the four from the bottom. He tried to recall their exact position. He needed to be farther across the screen. Frantically he maneuvered himself, then froze upright against the cliff face as he heard the *pow-pow-pow-pow* of the four shots.

He had gotten it right. Three passed to his right and one to his left. Then, as he heard the solitary shot from his left, the cliff opened before him in a dark hole. Thankfully he plunged into it.

His heart was thudding. He was shaking with relief. But the relief soon gave way to rage. Where was Mario? Why didn't the idiot hurry up and come after him? Every second counted: The sooner they started to destroy demons, the higher their score would be. The resentment Andrew felt at always being the one to be blasted into the game by Mario's hate was now compounded by a new fear.

He's not coming! he thought in panic. He's gone away and left me! I'll never get out of here!

In his mind's eye he could see Mario pocketing the gun and walking calmly out of the room, out of the house, and away forever.

He tried to reassure himself. There's no danger, he reasoned. The program will take care of everything.

He tried to hear its voice, but it was silent. It did not say "Welcome!" or "Well done!" It said nothing. There was no sound at all apart from the electronic pulse of the game, pounding faster and faster in time with Andrew's heart. As he crouched helplessly in the utter blackness, a dreadful chill began to steal over him. He was afraid and lonely. He had never felt like this before, and he hated the feeling. He should have been a powerful demon hunter, and instead he was hiding like a worm in the ground.

Then he began to feel guilty. This is how Ben must have felt, he thought. And he was in here for hours. I didn't realize how horrible it must have been for him. I thought he was just being a wimp. I did it to him. I put him here. And now Mario's done it to me.

Fear and guilt together began to erode his normal confidence. His throat felt thick and his eyes were stinging

unaccountably. In spite of himself, he began to despair.
His only consolation was in cursing Mario and planning
revenge. The bastard! he thought. Just the sort of ratlike
thing he would do! What an idiot I was ever to get involved
with him! I'll get even with him! I'll fix him good when I
see him! He's got one coming to him!

His heart gave a lurch. He could feel someone in the
tunnel with him. There was the shape of a person, even
darker than the darkness, and the glimmer of a white
face. He held his breath: Was it Mario or a space demon?
Could the game have changed to allow the demons into
the tunnels? If it had, he was lost. He had a sudden vivid
memory of the dream he'd had that morning. He cried
out. It was almost a cry for help.

"Mars!"

A snigger that was unmistakably Mario's sounded right
in his ear. "Bet you nearly wet yourself, you little creep."
A sneering laugh followed. "Good joke, huh? Like that
one? Bet you thought you were stuck in here." He laughed
again.

Andrew was too angry to say anything.

"Too bad it's too dark to see your face. You should have
heard yourself—'Mars!'" he mimicked. "I thought you
were crying for your mommy."

"Give me the gun," said Andrew angrily. He reached
out and drew the copy from Mario.

Still laughing, Mario let him take it. "There you go,
wimp, get your little toy pistol. But *this* is the real thing!"
He waved his own. "This is the one that really counts. And
I'm the one who really counts! Don't forget that! Not you,
you rich, stuck-up jerk. You know what you are? You're
nothing. Without me you'd be dead meat. I had to come
in here and rescue you—without me you'd never get out

of here again. *Dead meat!*" They glided up through the tunnel toward the ring of light at the end, and as they came to the top, he reached back and tapped Andrew on the head. "Stay behind Mars," he mocked. "I'll take care of you." Then he leaped out wildly, the gun flashing.

Andrew followed him with loathing in his heart. He was amazed at the strength of the feeling: It was a passion of hatred. He would pay Mario back if it was the last thing he ever did. He would get even with him. He would kill him if he could.

The voice of the program spoke suddenly and unexpectedly in his ear. *Very good*, it said. *The game must be played. It must be played right to the bitter end. Then you will see what happens when the demons hit their target.*

The game was speeding up. The boys knew the sequence of the attacks, but it was getting harder and harder to respond quickly enough. It's not any smarter than us, Andrew kept telling himself. It's just that it's so much faster. They had to work together covering and standing in for each other. They cooperated in spite of their mutual hatred. It was the only way to survive the game—and the elation of outwitting the demons, the thrill of their combined skill and ingenuity, outweighed even the passionate dislike. But Andrew was furious at having been left to sweat in the tunnel for so long, and smarting with resentment at the contempt Mario had shown for him. In his mind lurked the idea that now he would find out what happened if a demon did get you.

It was hardly even a conscious decision—it seemed the logical thing to do in the face of the unrelenting onslaught—and yet he knew afterward that at some point he'd made a choice. There was a split second when he could change his pattern of defense slightly and hold back on the edge of the tunnel at a time when Mario was expecting him to be at his back, defending him. Mario, gun blazing, facing the other way, did not see the demon behind him until it was nearly on his back. He swung the gun around and fired instantly, but the menacing black figure had already blasted him. For a moment Andrew saw Mario's mouth open as an expression of horror and fury flashed across his face. Then the boy and the demon disappeared together.

Serves him right, Andrew thought savagely. He had it coming to him. He thought he was so smart.

He felt no remorse, just a deep satisfaction that he'd gotten even. As though concurring with this, the voice of the program spoke to him. *Excellent!* it said. *I am deeply grateful.*

Once again he felt the approval of the intelligence behind the game. It encouraged him. He felt he'd done what was expected of him, almost what he had been programmed to do. Programmed? What a strange word to use. He wondered why he'd thought that. Of course he wasn't being programmed. He was acting from his own free will. Or was he? Hadn't it seemed, at that vital moment, as if it was inevitable that he should hold back for the fraction of a second that meant the difference between life and death for Mario?

Andrew shivered. He couldn't work it all out now. He decided he didn't want to think about Mario. Anyway, he said to himself, he probably just whizzed back into the room again. I'll see him there as soon as I get out of here.

But now he had to get out. And the game was faster than ever, raised to greater heights by the skill of two players, although now there was only one to handle it. I'll never cope with the speed by myself, Andrew thought. I'll have to work out some other strategy.

As long as he stayed in the dark, he was safe—the demons could not reach him there. But the longer he stayed there, the longer it would take to kill the required number of demons to bring him to the top of the cliff. And the longer he stayed in the game, the greater the danger of something else happening. If Mario was in Andrew's room, he might come back into the game and catch up with him, or he could turn the computer off. Andrew's mother might come in and find Mario there, or she might come in and find nobody there (he could not decide which of these alternatives would be worse). He had to do something, and do it as quickly as possible.

He crept to the edge of the tunnel and listened. He could hear the pulse of the game, but there were other noises as well. He realized that he could identify them, and that they had their own rhythmic pattern. When a demon appeared on the cliff face, there was a muffled *wheeee*, and the sound of its weapon firing was *tktktktktk*. Listening he realized that there was enough time between the *wheeee* and the *tktktktktk* to fit in a blast from his own gun. The shots from each demon had to go in a straight line across the cliff, either vertically or horizontally, but he, using the tunnels to come out above or below them, could use his gun diagonally. He crouched in the dark and listened until he had the rhythm going through his head like a song. When he finally made his first move, it was like being in a dance. Out of the darkness as soon as he heard the *wheeee*; *pow* went his own gun; back into the darkness while the *tktktktktk* went past; and then into the light again. He did not dare think about it—there was no time to think. He simply had to trust his reflexes and let it happen.

There was no question of wiping out the waves of demons as he and Mario had done before. He had to pick them off with agonizing slowness, one by one. It seemed that hours passed before at last the noises stopped altogether. He felt only a faint pulse in the blessed silence as the starry sky wheeled overhead and the cliff top formed beneath his feet. The same pulse beat achingly in his head as he passed through the screen and back into his room.

His hand was empty. His gun, he remembered, was only a replica. The room was empty too. There was no sign of Mario. Andrew didn't feel anything in particular about that. He didn't feel anything much. He was exhausted, profoundly relieved to be back in his own room, and curiously depressed. He thought vaguely to himself, I've had enough of this game. I don't think I'll play it anymore.

He crumpled up the note he had written earlier and threw it in the wastepaper basket. Then he switched the computer off. He lay down on his bed, pulled the quilt up over his head, and immediately fell asleep.

15

Earlier the same afternoon Mr. Russell had kept his promise to come and see Elaine in the gym.

"We can't do much," Elaine said after she and Ben had

done some tumbling. "We could do a lot more if we were able to use the equipment."

"You'd need supervision for that," their teacher said. "I'm probably already stretching the rules letting you use the gym. It's only because I trust you to know what you're doing and not break any bones. Anyway, you should be going to gymnastics classes. You'd learn a lot more than just practicing on your own. You've certainly got what it takes."

Elaine didn't say anything, but she gave him a look that said, "It's impossible for me to go to classes. I'm doing the best I can."

Mr. Russell stood thinking for a moment. "Perhaps we could get a class going here. I know a couple of people who are gym instructors. I'll sound them out, see if they have any time available. Leave it to me. I won't make any promises, but we'll see if we can't get something going next term."

"Thanks," Elaine said. She didn't want to get too excited, but it sounded like a great idea. She often felt frustrated because she was not learning anything new. She was just messing around. She had not forgotten the promise she'd made to herself in Andrew Hayford's house. She was determined to make something of her life and she wanted to start as early as possible. If she was going to be famous and successful, she had a long way to go.

"Why don't you put on a show for the class at the end of the term?" Mr. Russell went on. "There's still a couple of weeks to get it ready. You could work on it with Ben and John."

"I wouldn't know what to do," Elaine protested.

"I'm sure that inventive brain of yours can come up

with something. How about a science fiction story?"

Hey, she thought to herself, that was below the belt! But she said, "I suppose I could give it a try."

"Good! I think you should have some musical effects, too, don't you? You could ask Linda to play the piano for you."

"I could," she agreed, not very enthusiastically. She was thinking, This guy's too quick on his feet for me!

"Good for you!"

Elaine shook her head ruefully as she watched him leave.

"What's the matter?" Ben asked. "You didn't sound very enthusiastic about the gymnastics class."

"I'll be enthusiastic about it when it happens," she replied.

"Oh, you don't know him. If he says that much, it'll happen, you'll see. He'll make it happen."

"Anyway," Elaine said, "he's gone and stuck me with Linda. That takes all the fun out of doing a show."

"Yeah, what was all that about?"

"He thinks we should be friends. He thinks we'd be good for each other." Elaine made a face. "It's always the things that are good for you that are the worst."

"You'll have to do it now," John said from where he was sitting on the mat. "He more or less told you to."

"I don't *have* to do it," Elaine said. "I'll do it if I feel like it. I'm not sure yet if I feel like it or not."

"We could do that dance you and Ben can do—you know?" John suggested. "That way we could just use a tape, and we wouldn't have to ask Linda."

Elaine was not going to commit herself. "I'll think about it," was all she would say. "I'll tell you later. Right now— less talk, more action!" She jumped up and turned a somersault in the air.

When she came down, her face was greenish-white and she swayed on her feet.

"What's wrong?" asked Ben, startled. "Did you go over too fast?"

She put out a hand, grabbed his wrist, and whispered fiercely so John wouldn't hear. "You know what made Andrew yell out in the classroom this afternoon? I saw it too. I saw the same reflection in the window. And I just saw it again when I flipped over. Those black things aren't cracks! They're getting bigger! They're growing!"

"I know," Ben said reluctantly. He had been trying to forget what he'd seen in the classroom. "I saw them this afternoon too. They're growing into space demons."

Elaine gave her head a strong shake. "If only you could actually *see* them," she said. "They're driving me mad! You can't quite see them, and when you look around they run away. You just catch sight of them sometimes. And they're always there!"

"Something's making them grow," Ben said.

They stared at each other. The unease and misgivings each had privately been trying to ignore would not be ignored any longer. They came flooding in. Elaine turned even paler. Ben felt his heart begin to race.

John looked from one to the other, puzzled. "What the heck's the matter with you two?"

"John," Ben said, "has your brother been going over to Andrew's?"

"Every day this week," John answered. "Strange, isn't it? You wouldn't have thought they'd be friends."

"They're not friends," Ben said grimly. "What's Mario been like lately?"

"How do you mean?"

"Well, is he acting funny?"

"He always acts funny," John said. "He doesn't know what normal is."

"Is he worse than usual though?" Elaine asked impatiently. "Andrew definitely is. He looked like he was cracking up this afternoon. Mr. Russell was about to send for a straitjacket."

John thought. "I'd say he's been really bad this week," he said slowly. "Yeah, come to think of it, it's been one of the worst weeks ever. He had a real blow-out with Dad last night. Dad tried to belt him one, but Mars's too fast for him now. He ran out and he didn't come in till after midnight. I let him in—Mom's working the late shift. This morning Dad was off to work at six, so they didn't see each other, but Dad said last night he's had it with Mars. If he gives them any more trouble, Dad says he'll just throw him out of the house. When I told Mars that this morning, he said, 'He won't get the chance. I'll run away first.' What's that got to do with Andrew?"

"Johnny, can you see anything weird out of the corner of your eye?" Elaine interrupted.

John rolled his eyes backward and made a face. "Nothing that's not usually there. What's up with you two? Why all the funny questions?"

Ben and Elaine exchanged looks. Elaine said lightly, "Oh, nothing really. Why don't you go and find Dad and ask him how much longer he's going to be?"

"Okay," John agreed.

When he was out of the gym, Ben said, "Do you know what's happening?"

"Not a clue," Elaine answered. "What do you think?"

"Andrew and Mario are obviously playing the game every day. The more they play, the more hate they're generating. It's spilling out all over the place. And the more hate there is around, the more the demon things have to feed on. So they're getting bigger. They're getting more real."

"How far do you think they have to go?" Elaine asked nervously.

"They're looking too real for me already!" Ben said.

"Well, what do you think happens next?" Elaine was feeling so nervous that she did a back flip to steady herself.

"I don't know. They're pursuing us for some reason. They're after us because we've been through the game. They must need us for something."

"Neither of us wanted to go into that game," Elaine said angrily. "Andrew put us there. I hate him for that!"

A little tremor ran through the air. The space demons in the gym became a fraction bigger. Neither Ben nor Elaine noticed it.

John reappeared at the door. "Your dad's going to be another half hour," he announced. "And I've got to go now. It's nearly six o'clock."

"I'd better go too," Ben said. "I promised I wouldn't be late. Darren's in a debate tonight, and the whole family's got to turn out to cheer."

"What's he debating?" said John with interest.

"Whether artificial intelligence is potentially superior to the human brain."

"What's that mean?"

"Whether computers are smarter than people," Ben explained. "Darren's defending it."

"He'd better lose!" Elaine said with feeling.

"Darren never loses, even when he's wrong," Ben said gloomily.

The boys left together and Elaine went to look for her father. He was still vacuuming, so she went and sat in the

office and talked to Mrs. Fields, who was finishing up some
typing. They had become quite friendly since Mr. Taylor
had started doing the cleaning. Sometimes Elaine helped
run off stencils or did photocopying for the next day, and
sometimes Mrs. Fields would make her a cup of cocoa
before she went home and give her a piece of homemade
cake. Elaine enjoyed being in the office. It was somewhere
warm and cozy to sit on cold days.

"I'm taking the rest of the week off," Mrs. Fields explained. "My daughter's getting married on Saturday, and
I've got so much to do. Could you fold these and put them
in the envelopes for me, Elly?"

Her fingers flashed over the typewriter keys while she
talked. Elaine remembered the first day she had been in
the office. A lot certainly had happened since then. And
things *had* worked out. She realized with surprise that her
father had been right. If he hadn't been working as the
school janitor, she would never have been able to use the
gym with Ben. John was turning out to be not so bad after
all. And she was sitting here with someone who she knew
liked her. She realized that she was less lonely than she'd
been for a long time. She actually had three people she
could almost call friends. Then, turning her head to reach
another pile of letters, she felt a thud of fear as *something*
moved away out of her vision. Just when everything's
going so well, she thought in desperation. If it weren't for
those shadows I would almost be happy. That creep
Andrew Hayford! He's spoiled everything!

"Mind you, I don't know what I'll do with myself when
it's over," Mrs. Fields said, still talking about the wedding.
"This is my last child to go! The house'll be so quiet
without her. Seven children we've raised in it. Four of our

own, and three foster children. Les and I will be rattling around like a pair of peas!"

She made an exclamation of annoyance, tore the letter she had started out of the typewriter, and put in another piece of paper. "Serves me right for chattering," she said. "I addressed it to Dr. and Mrs. Hayford; I should have just put 'Mrs.' They were talking about it in the staff room this morning. The Hayfords have separated. Andrew's father's gone to live in the city."

"Andrew Hayford?" Elaine said in astonishment. She could not believe her ears. She had always imagined that someone like Andrew would have the ideal family.

"Oh, I probably shouldn't be gossiping," Mrs. Fields went on. "Keep it to yourself, will you, Elaine? It's such a shame though, such a lovely family. No wonder poor little Andrew has been looking a bit miserable lately."

Poor little Andrew! thought Elaine. That put him in an entirely different light. It was the last way she would have described him.

She realized she was actually pleased by this unexpected piece of information. Serves him right, she thought with satisfaction. Conceited thing! Now he knows what it feels like! So his dad walked out on them, just like Mom did! I bet it was because he couldn't stand Andrew. And next time I see him, I'll tell him! She was so busy savoring the feeling of triumph that she forgot all about the gym class. She only remembered it when she was riding home with her father. By then it had become real enough to seem like a definite event, and she could dare to talk about it.

"Mr. Russell is going to get a gymnastics class together next term," she said to him. "It's going to be great."

"Don't get your hopes up," her father said without

taking his eyes off the road. "We won't be here next term."

All her hopes seemed to drain from her at once. She flung herself against him, gripping his arm. "What do you mean?"

"Watch it!" he said sharply. The truck swerved, and the driver of a car in the next lane honked in alarm.

I hope we hit it! Elaine thought savagely with a fraction of her mind. The rest of her was going wild. "What do you mean?" she said again. "Why won't we be here next term?"

"I've practically finished the house, love. And the regular janitor's coming back to school next week, so they won't need me anymore. I thought we'd leave here and move on. I hear there's more work farther south."

"But I don't want to move on! I want to stay right here!"

She could not believe how terrible she was feeling about it. I did it again, she thought furiously. I never meant to. I didn't know I was doing it. I put down roots. I made friends. I forgot we never stay anywhere.

The pickup pulled into the driveway. Elaine leaped out and slammed the door in rage. She ran into the house and looked around. How could she not have noticed the changes that had been taking place in it? The kitchen was finished. Pine benches and dark-blue cupboards, pale gleaming cork tiles on the floor, all stared insolently at her. Outside, where there had been a quagmire, there were now neat bricks under a latticework arbor. It wasn't a dump anymore. It was starting to look like a beautiful house, worth its entire purchase price. It mocked her. "You poor idiot," it said. "Suckered again!"

Her father had followed her in. He looked around, too, but with pride and self-satisfaction. "Looking pretty good, I reckon," he said. "I've just got to sand all the woodwork and the floors, and fix the front yard up a bit, and then we'll be done. It's given us a good base for the winter. Jeff will be pleased when he gets back. I suppose he'll want to move in himself by the end of the month. He paid a lot for the place, but it's going to make a beautiful home."

"I want to live in it," Elaine said. "Why can't it be ours?"

Her father shrugged his shoulders and went to put the kettle on. As far as he was concerned, there was nothing to discuss.

I'm in agony, Elaine thought. And he doesn't even care. But I'm not going to give in this time. I am not going to be bulldozed anymore. I've had enough of it!

"Dad," she said, trying to talk calmly. "I really do think we should stay here. I need to take some gymnastics classes. Mr. Russell thinks I'm pretty good. I'd like to take ballet too. I like the school. I've made friends. I'll die if we have to go."

Her father was making cocoa. He handed her a mug. "Elly," he said, "be reasonable! I need to find work. If I don't work, we don't eat. The work here has run out. We'll have to move on somewhere. We can't stay in this house— the guy who owns it wants to live in it. And I'd like a bit of sunshine. This cold weather's killing me. You'll enjoy traveling on. You always do."

"I don't!" she cried. "I just want to stay put somewhere. I want to have a real home! I'll never get to be anyone if we're always bouncing around. I'll just end up a weirdo like you!"

She looked at the mug in her hand, wondered why on earth he was giving her cocoa at a time like this, and hurled it to the ground. The mug bounced several times on the cork tiles, spilling cocoa everywhere.

Quickly her father reached out and smacked her hard

on the shoulder. "You watch the way you talk to me!" he shouted. "I deserve some respect from you! I'm your father, remember?"

"I wish you weren't," she cried. As soon as she'd said it, she wished she hadn't, but it was too late to take it back, and anyway she couldn't stop herself from going on. She was scared of him, but she was too angry to care. "I'm not surprised Mom left you. I would, too, if I'd have been her. I just wish she'd taken me with her!"

"Taken you with her!" he roared. "That's the last thing she would have done! She wanted to be free, that's what she kept saying. She didn't want to be anyone's mother. Even when you were little, she never cared for you."

Elaine looked at him in horror. "That's not true!" she said.

"It *is* true. It wasn't your fault. You were born too early— you nearly died—and somehow all of it was too much for your mom. You had to stay in the hospital for weeks, and when you finally came home, she acted strange. She couldn't cope, and she got upset when you cried. Well, that wasn't your fault, of course, but your mother couldn't handle it. And then, when you started to grow up, she seemed to resent having you around more and more. She kept saying she'd gotten married too young, never had any life of her own. She needed to find out who she was, all that sort of thing." His voice was bitter, and Elaine could sense the anger and frustration behind the words. He turned away from her and put his empty mug in the sink. "She didn't want to be anyone's mother, and she certainly didn't want to be anyone's wife, so she ran away," he said heavily. "Thinking it over I'm surprised she stayed around as long as she did."

He turned back toward her. His face was set and his

blue eyes were serious. "Don't yell at me," he warned. "I've done everything for you, with precious little help from anyone. And I'm going to go on looking after you, that's for sure, but I've got to lead the sort of life *I* like, and you've got to fit in with that. Now clear up that mess and stop acting like a five-year-old."

Elaine was still angry, but his words had taken the edge off her rage and had plunged her into another sort of turmoil, both confirming and allaying her deepest fears. Her mother had not wanted her. She had never cared for her. She had run away from her. The truth of the words made Elaine want to die, but at the same time, to have them said took away their power to hurt her. She realized that the truth faced up to was far less dangerous than the truth suspected and avoided—and he had said, too, that it was not her fault. . . .

She looked at her father in confusion.

"Elly," he said gently, his anger also abating. He put his hand out to her.

Elaine felt dangerously near tears, and she knew that if she cried, that would be the end of the argument. Her father would give her comfort and love, but she would then feel vulnerable. She gritted her teeth and muttered through them, "Go away! I hate you!"

His hand dropped and he turned away from her.

Her rage returned. She no longer felt in danger of tears. "I am not going to go," she muttered to herself as she fetched a cloth and wiped the floor. She was hanging on to the words as though they were a lifeline across a flooded river. As long as she kept saying them, no one would be able to force her to do what she didn't want to. "I am not going to go. I am not going to go."

Yet all the time the sight of her father, so large and so

angry, filled her with despair. A part of her knew that no matter what she said, he would still do just what he wanted. He always did. He would never alter his lifestyle to suit her. He would continue to bulldoze his way through life, and she would continue to trail after him, a disposable person with no rights and no place in the world.

Darkness had fallen during the argument and the curtainless windows reflected the scene inside the kitchen. Elaine had been too angry to notice the black cracks for a while, but now she caught sight of one behind her to the left. As she instinctively moved her head to get rid of it, she saw something moving in the reflection.

There was no doubt about it, it was just what she had seen in the gym—a space demon, facing her—but even larger and more real. She gasped. Its dark eyes were looking straight at her. It was calm, impassive, and unbelievably menacing.

It's going to get me, she thought in terror. It's after me. I can't handle this. I've got too much to cope with already. I can't handle any of it anymore. I feel like killing someone! I feel like killing everyone! It's all Andrew Hayford's fault. I'll murder him!

The demon grew a little more.

Elaine went to bed and lay awake in the dark, her eyes wide open, her mind in turmoil. The room had become familiar to her, with its high, ornate ceiling and arched windows, the veranda outside, and beyond it the dark, wild shrubs through which headlights flashed intermittently as cars passed along the street. She ached with affection for it. She did not want to leave it.

"I won't let them do it to me," she reassured herself aloud. "I'm not going to be pushed around anymore. I'm not going to be hurt anymore. I'm not going to take any more. This is it! I'm going to be in control. From now on if anyone's going to be doing any pushing around, it's going to be me!"

She felt hatred simmering inside her. She lay there feeding it, fanning it, until it was positively boiling. It made her feel strong and powerful. For a long time she lay awake, letting it grow and grow. When at last she fell asleep, she had a vivid and terrifying dream.

She was standing by the monkey bars in the school playground. There was nobody else around, and she thought she would do some exercising. She felt the usual thrill at the skill and control of her body as she swung herself around. She was hanging upside down when she heard a laugh, and a voice said, "Look at the chimpanzee!" Turning her head, she saw it was Andrew Hayford, but he had dark hair and chalk-white skin. He was holding something round and black in his hand, and when he raised it, liquid darkness, like ink, began to pour out of it. The darkness began to cover everything and as she watched, unable to move, it rose all around her and drowned her. Worst of all, Andrew watched her the whole time, making no effort to help her. When she finally drowned, the last sound she heard was his echoing laughter.

16

Andrew was having the same dream. After he had painted Elaine into darkness, he went to look for someone else. He found Ben and John Ferrone in the gym, and he watched dispassionately while the darkness streamed out of the gun and engulfed them. The gun filled in the background and obliterated anyone who was standing against it. It was very satisfying. Next he painted out Mr. Russell in his classroom, along with Elaine's father, who happened to walk in, sticking his nose into other people's business, as usual. Then Andrew found himself at home. He could hear his parents arguing in the kitchen. He felt intensely annoyed with them. Why did they keep spoiling his life with their fighting? He opened the kitchen door and saw them silhouetted against the gleaming white and stainless steel background. He wiped them out.

"Andrew!" his mother called from somewhere behind the blackness. "Andrew!"

He ignored her. He wanted her to disappear forever but she wouldn't be quiet.

"Andrew!"

He opened his eyes. The darkness receded. It was daytime.

"What time is it?" he asked. The room was quite light, and birds were making a late sort of noise in the trees outside.

"It's after nine," his mother said. "You've slept for hours and hours. You were asleep when I came up to tell you dinner was ready last night."

Andrew realized he was still in his clothes. "I suppose I'd better get up," he said, making no move to get out of bed. He felt very reluctant to face the day.

"There's no hurry," his mother answered. "You don't have to go to school today. I'm taking you in to see Dr. Freeman, but that's not till eleven o'clock."

Andrew looked at her in surprise. "Who's Dr. Freeman? And why do I have to see him? I'm not sick."

"You haven't been quite yourself lately. I'm a bit worried about you. I just thought it would help you to have a talk to somebody—other than me, I mean."

His mother did not look at him while she spoke. She was tidying up his room, putting clothes in drawers, and straightening up things that didn't really need it.

"A talk about what?" Andrew said slowly.

"Oh, just about how you feel at the moment, the things that are bothering you, that sort of thing." He could see her reflection in the mirror. Their eyes met briefly. She smiled anxiously and looked away.

Andrew did not smile back. "Nothing's bothering me," he said. He could feel anger beginning to build inside him. Why didn't she just leave him alone? "Who is this Freeman guy anyway?"

His mother picked up a pile of magazines and began to arrange them on the bookshelf. "He's a friend of your father's—they did their training together. He's . . . well, I suppose you'd call him a child psychiatrist."

"A psychiatrist! Mom, do you think I'm going nuts or something?"

"Of course I don't. But you don't seem very happy, and . . . I just think it would do you good to talk to someone about it, that's all."

She came and sat down on the bed and patted his cheek.

"Put some clean clothes on," she said gently. "I'll make breakfast." She gave him another anxious smile, got up, and went out of the room, closing the door carefully behind her.

Her gentleness unsettled Andrew. He wanted her to be unreasonable and angry, so he could have something positive to hate, so he could blame her for the consuming hostility he was feeling. He frowned, biting his lip. His head ached with a persistent thudding that reminded him of Space Demons. He couldn't quite remember what had happened. His glance fell on the silent computer. Something had gone wrong, something had made him not want to play the game anymore. He couldn't quite recall if it had really happened or if he had dreamed it. His brain seemed to have gone on strike, like after the time when he had first played the game with Mario. . . . That was it! Mario! Something had happened to Mario. But what? Where was he?

"He's probably okay," he said aloud, trying to convince himself. "He probably just went home after we finished playing, and I've forgotten it. I don't seem to be thinking too straight at the moment. What's wrong with me? Why do I feel so awful?"

On top of his chest of drawers there was a photo of him taken at the beach last summer with his father and mother. He and his father had been windsurfing; the pink-and-white sail of the board contrasted sharply with their brown skin. They all looked happy and carefree. He couldn't believe they were the same family. Dad's away for weeks at a time, he thought, Mom's always crying about something or other, and I'm . . . I'm . . . what am I?

Whatever he was, he knew he was not all right. He looked from the photo to his reflection in the mirror. He had grown much paler, and he looked insubstantial and transparent. As though I'm fading away, he thought. As he looked back wistfully at the photo, fear gripped him in the pit of his stomach.

They were standing behind him. He could see their reflections in the mirror. He did not dare turn around. The demons stared hard at him in the mirror. They were more real than he had ever seen them, far more real than they were in the game. They were almost fully three-dimensional.

He could not move; he could not do anything. He was completely paralyzed.

"Andrew, how are you doing? Breakfast is ready." The door opened and his mother came in. The demons slowly shrank and faded. Turning his head, Andrew saw that there was no longer anything behind him, but a little patch of darkness that swung away as he turned, and then swung back, to hang on the periphery of his vision and haunt him.

Under his mother's anxious eyes he ate breakfast mechanically, hardly daring to move his head. When they went outside to get in the car, he saw something else that unsettled him even further. He stopped short and said, "Oh, cripes!"

"What is it?" His mother's voice was quick and worried. She followed his gaze. He was looking at a black bike that was lying on its side in the flower bed.

"Isn't that your friend . . . that boy's bicycle?" she said. "Did he leave it behind yesterday? Pick it up out of the flower bed, Andrew, it's squashing the daffodils."

That is definitely Mario's bike, Andrew was thinking. That's where he left it yesterday. But he would never have gone home without it. He'd as soon have left one of his legs here. That means he didn't go home. . . .

He ground his fingernails into his palms. He was not going to think about it anymore. With an enormous effort he held his mind completely still. He did not think about anything at all. He picked up the bike, carefully wheeled it into the garage, and leaned it up alongside his own. Then he got into the car. They drove into the city without speaking.

Dr. Freeman was a handsome man with thick brown hair and blue eyes that had a perpetual twinkle in them. He looked younger than he was, and he had the engaging habit of concentrating totally on whoever it was he was talking to as though he or she were the most important person in the world. Andrew found it hard to believe he was a psychiatrist. He looked more like a TV actor. Even though he wore glasses, Andrew suspected they were more of a prop than a necessity. Dr. Freeman looked over them quizzically, took them off to appear more intimate, and waved them in the air to emphasize a point. He couldn't possibly need them for seeing through, Andrew thought.

Dr. Freeman put his glasses back on his nose and looked over them at Andrew.

"Well, tell me some more about yourself, Andrew. You're in, let me see, seventh grade? How do you like school?"

"Not much," Andrew said. "Does anyone?"

Dr. Freeman smiled. "What about friends? I imagine you've got quite a few?"

"I've got one very good friend, Ben Challis. He's my best friend . . . but I haven't been seeing much of him lately." Andrew realized as he said it that he was kind of sad about it: He missed Ben.

"Who do you spend your time with now?" Dr. Freeman asked casually.

"No one, really."

"Your mother mentioned someone new," the doctor went on. Underneath his relaxed manner he was relentlessly insistent. "What's his name . . . ?"

"Mario," Andrew said. His heart was beginning to pound. He didn't want to think about Mario, but everyone was forcing him to. He frowned and looked nervously over his shoulder. There was nothing there, yet, but he was afraid that at any moment there would be. Dr. Freeman was watching him closely. He made a couple of notes on his pad. "What are you looking at?" he said.

"Sometimes I have the feeling that there's something creeping up on me," Andrew said. "It's something I can't quite see, but it's there. And sometimes I think I can see its reflection, in the mirror or in the window."

"Has that been going on for long?"

Andrew looked at the doctor carefully. His heart was pounding more and more, and his hands were sweating. He could feel panic sweeping over him. He wanted to tell somebody about it, but he knew nobody would believe him. Not only would they not believe him, they would think he was going crazy.

"You can tell me about it, Andrew. That's what I'm here for." Dr. Freeman's voice hit just the right note of calm friendliness.

Andrew took a deep breath. "My father brought a computer game back from overseas. It's called Space Demons." He paused, not sure how to go on.

"And you've been playing it a lot?" Dr. Freeman prompted.

"Yes."

"You like computer games?" When Andrew nodded, the doctor went on, "Do you play it on your own, or with a friend?"

"That's why Mario came . . . comes . . . around. I play it with him."

"Well, let's talk about Mario," said the doctor encouragingly. "Tell me what you like about him."

"I don't like anything about him," Andrew said violently. There was a little shimmer in the air behind him, as though something were thickening out. He jumped and bit his lip, and looked up desperately at Dr. Freeman.

"But you like to play the computer game with him. He must be a good player."

"Yeah, he's a good player, all right. He's one of the best." As he said it, Andrew remembered the admiration he had felt for Mario the first time he'd seen him play the game, admiration for his bravery and skill. How could you hate someone and admire him at the same time? The ambiguity of his feelings confused him, and in the confusion he lost hold of his refusal to think about what had happened to Mario. It all came back to him with a sickening rush. Mario had been shot. He was lost somewhere in the game. And it was Andrew's fault.

"Oh, God!" he said.

"Tell me what you're feeling now, Andrew," Dr. Freeman said calmly.

Tell you what I'm feeling! Andrew thought. No way! If I told you what I was feeling right now, you'd cart me right off to the funny farm! Thoughts were rushing through his head with the speed of electronic impulses. His brain had gone from deep freeze to boiling point. It had put itself into a crazy random access pattern and was throwing emotions and schemes around like confetti. Terror was there, and guilt, disgust at himself, and horror, but luckily they were not the only things. There were also resolve, clarity, decisiveness, the same sort of razor-edged coolness that you had to have to be a champion demon hunter.

The game's not finished, he thought. There's more to play. I've got to get back into it one more time.

"Andrew," the doctor said, quietly but insistently, "I'd like you to tell me what you're feeling. Don't be ashamed of anything, or think you have to hide anything. You can say whatever you like to me."

"I'd like to go now," Andrew said, getting up abruptly. "I've just thought of something very important I've got to do. I've got to get home."

A look of frustration passed fleetingly across Dr. Freeman's face, but he hid it quickly under a professional smile. "Very well." He stood up too. "We'll leave it there for today. I want you to have a couple of tests before you go, blood tests and so on. I'll see you again on . . ." He consulted his appointment book. "Let's say in a week's time. And Andrew," he added, putting his arm on Andrew's shoulder as they walked to the door, "just remember, we all have to face up to things we don't like. We can't run away from things forever."

I know that! Andrew thought with feeling. But I don't think you and I are talking about the same thing!

When the blood tests were finished, Andrew went back to Dr. Freeman's room.

"I've got some pills I want you to take," the doctor said. "We'll see what difference they make in your behavior

pattern, and we'll talk again next week. Take care, and
watch those computer games. We don't want you turning
into a computer!"

"I'm not taking them," Andrew said when he and his
mother were in the car again. She was concentrating on
backing out of the parking space; another car was waiting
right behind her to take the space, and she didn't have
much room. She hated these multistory parking garages.
They made her feel shut in and frightened, and driving
around and around in spirals in the semidarkness was a
nightmare. Then she had to stop at the exit and find the
right change. As she fumbled in her purse, the driver
behind her honked the horn and made her more nervous
and clumsy than ever. At last they were out in the daylight.
She sighed and said, "What was that, darling?"

Andrew was seething with impatience. He knew with
absolute certainty that what he had to do was get home
and start playing Space Demons all over again. He had
switched the computer off so the game would revert to the
start, but even if it still had been at the vortex level it
would not have helped him, because the original gun had
disappeared with Mario. Without a gun he had no way of
getting back into the game. He would have to play through
all the stages, go into the game all those times again, until
he activated the vortex and came out with the gun. Before,
the whole process had taken him days. He had no idea
how long it would take now, but he had to get started. He
had a furious sense of urgency. He could not rest until he
had put things right again.

"I'm not going to take any pills, Mom." How could he
take pills, which would almost certainly be sedatives? He

needed to be at his sharpest and most wide-awake. To take any pills now would be disaster.

His mother stole a look at him as they waited for the light to change. His face was pale and set, and he had a dark look around his eyes. There was definitely something wrong with him. What could be happening to her cheerful, charming, confident son? She blamed herself bitterly.

"Did you like Dr. Freeman?" she asked tentatively.

"Actually, I thought he was a jerk! And he was way off track about me! There's nothing wrong with me, and I'm not taking his stupid pills!"

"Just take them till next week," she pleaded. "Dr. Freeman wants to help you and he knows best. You must do what he says."

That's what adults always say, Andrew thought. They always want to help you and they always know best. But they don't know anything at all about Space Demons.

As soon as they got home, he ran inside the house and up to his room. His mother followed him, protesting about the pills.

"All right, all right," Andrew said to get her off his back. "I'll take them. Give them to me."

He put two in his mouth and pretended to swallow them, but in fact he tucked them inside his cheek. Then he threw himself down on his bed and said, "I think I'll go back to sleep again. I'm really tired."

"The pills might make you drowsy," his mother said. "Do you want some lunch first?"

"No thanks," Andrew replied. As soon as she was out of the room, he spat out the pills and hid them under his pillow. Then he curled up with his face toward the wall and pretended to be asleep. He thought his mother would probably tiptoe in later to check on him. He wanted her to think he was asleep; then she would leave him alone for a couple of hours at least.

After about twenty minutes he heard the door open quietly. He breathed deeply and slowly. The door closed again, and he heard her footsteps fade away down the stairs.

Quickly he got up and locked the door of his room. Then he sat down in front of the computer. He took a deep breath. He realized that he was trembling. He turned on the computer and pressed the start button. When the deep blue of the first level of Space Demons came up on the screen, he couldn't believe how harmless and innocent it looked. It seemed like a lifetime ago that he had played it for the first time. He summoned up all his powers of concentration and skill and began to play.

The stages of the game remained exactly the same— and yet the feel of it was different. Before, he had felt that the program was on his side, helping him, leading him on. Now it seemed to be against him, hindering him whenever it could. He was having to fight it at every stage. And it was much harder to concentrate, because he was always aware of something in the room with him, looming up behind him, leaning over his shoulder. The demons on the screen and the demons in the room seemed to be controlled by the same brain; they seemed to be working together, trying to prevent him from getting back in the game. It was taking him much longer to play through even the easy stages of the game. He was moving too slowly, thinking too sluggishly, making too many mistakes.

This is no good, he thought in desperation. I'm never going to do it. He stared in frustration at the screen in front of him. It had just returned once again to deep blue. "There must be a way," he said aloud. "There must be something I can do. I know I can play the game. I know I'm good enough at it." He could feel anger boiling up inside him, but the angrier he grew the less he was able to concentrate. Anger wasn't helping at all; in fact, it seemed to be making things worse. He realized that the more his frustration and anger grew, the more real the black figures behind him became, the more they seemed to menace him, and the harder the game seemed.

The game responds to hate, he thought. And that's what's feeding those demons. Hate, anger, all those things are making them grow. The game is feeding off that energy in the person playing it, and sending that into the demons, into its "children," as it calls them. Ugh, it's horrible, it gives me the creeps! I wish I could just give the whole thing away.

But even as he thought that, he knew that it was out of the question. The game had to be played out now until the end. Strangely, this realization reassured him slightly. "It *is* only a game," he said to himself. "No matter how smart it seems, it's only a program. It has to follow its own rules. If it responds to hate, then it must . . . it must *not respond when there's no hate!*"

The thought penetrated his mind like a tiny beam of light through a pinhole on a blind. He looked at it dispassionately. His anger began to drain away. It was not enough to give him hope, but it was at least something to start with. It would have to do.

Mars, he thought, I'm sorry!

Immediately there rose in his mind the outrage and fury he had felt when Mario had kept him waiting in the tunnels. He deserved whatever happened to him!

No! Don't think like that! Let it go!

Refuse to hate!

The pain of refusing was immense. It was like cutting out a part of himself. At his back the demons solidified.

He kept his mind steady.

Refuse to hate!

The minute light became almost imperceptibly larger.

He was concentrating on it so hard that he got through the asteroid bombardment without thinking. The number 9,876 flashed up, and he tensed as the demons began to pour across the screen.

"It's only a game," he repeated to himself. "I've done this dozens of times before. I can handle it."

The feeling of oppression lifted slightly. The feeling that there was something right behind him lessened.

It's working, he thought. I'm going to get there.

Patiently and calmly he played on and on.

17

Elaine woke with a sensation of panic. For a few moments she lay in bed wondering where she was and if she was alive or dead. The nightmare of drowning in darkness was still vivid in her mind. It filled her with fury toward Andrew.

Just wait till I see him today! she thought. I'm really going to fix him!

Then she remembered the fight she'd had with her

father the night before. It made her feel worse and worse. The blackness of the dream still seemed to be engulfing her, filling her with rage against everyone and everything.

There was a terrible racket outside. She got out of bed and opened the door. Her father had started sanding the woodwork in the hallway. The air was full of grit and dust that stung her eyes and throat. The house had become a place to get away from—she couldn't get out of it fast enough.

She got dressed and tried to braid her tangled hair, wrenching at it angrily, making her eyes sting even more. I must get it cut, she thought to herself, but I don't know where to go, and I don't have money, and there's no way I'm going to ask Dad today!

The noise of the sander stopped and her father came to the doorway, "Do you want some breakfast, Elaine?"

She knew from his voice that he was sorry for being angry, but she wasn't ready to make up yet, she was still too angry. Besides, making up would be the same as giving in. Sullenly, without looking at him, she said, "I'm not hungry." She picked up her knapsack from the floor, pushed past him, and opened the front door. Patchy rain was falling, driven by a southwesterly wind.

"I'll drive you to school," he offered. "You'll get soaked if you walk in this." He went to look for his keys.

"I don't want you to!" Elaine shouted back into the house, and she ran out through the wet shrubs into the street.

There was no sign of John outside. I must be really late, she thought. He's given up waiting. But as she hurried around the corner, she saw him coming toward her from the direction of the high school. When he saw her, he broke into a run.

"Elaine," he said urgently as he came up to her, "have you seen Mario?" When she shook her head he went on, "He didn't come home all night. And I've just been up to the high school—there's no sign of him there. What the heck do you think's happened to him?"

"How should I know?" Elaine said. She had enough problems of her own, without being expected to worry about Mario as well. "He's probably just stayed out for the night to give you all a scare."

John looked at her, his eyes big and pathetic. "He threatened to run away. Do you think he has?"

"Does it matter?" Elaine said crossly. "Sounds to me like you'd all be much happier if he did."

"Don't say that," John said. "He's my brother! What if something awful's happened to him? Suppose he's been kidnapped? Or had an accident?"

"Don't worry about him," Elaine said. "He can look after himself. What do your parents think?"

"They don't know," John said. "They just thought he went out early this morning—his bike's not there. But I know he never came in last night. I was lying awake most of the night waiting for him, and he never came home. Something's happened to him, I know it. He's in some kind of terrible trouble."

Elaine shivered. She thought again of the blackness of the dream, and somebody laughing . . . Andrew Hayford! Mario had been going over to Andrew's every day to play the computer game, and now John said he had not come home all night. Just as, before, Ben had not come home from Andrew's. . . .

Somewhere on the edge of her vision a dark shape moved menacingly.

"Oh, no," she said in dismay.

"What is it?"

"Let's go and find Ben," Elaine said. "I need to talk to him."

But before she could find him, the bell rang and they had to line up outside their classroom. Ben arrived just as the students were walking in, and Elaine had no time to talk to him. She watched anxiously to see if Andrew would turn up—he had been late so often recently that it was not until well into the first period that she could be sure he was not coming at all. This made her even more uneasy. She kept trying to tell herself that it had nothing to do with her, and that if Mario and Andrew were in some kind of trouble, it was their own fault.

I don't know who's the worst, she thought to herself. Probably Andrew. At least Mario doesn't pretend to be nice. They're a really mean pair. I'm not surprised they teamed up together. I hope they've both disappeared for good, she thought, and let her mind dwell on what might be happening to them at that moment. Whatever it was, it served them right!

Behind her dark shapes shimmered and thickened.

Elaine twisted and turned in her chair. The minutes dragged by till recess. As soon as the bell rang, she jumped up and dashed out of the classroom. Outside Linda Schulz came up to her.

"Hi, Elly," she said.

Elaine looked at her in surprise. Was Linda actually being friendly? "What do you want?" she asked warily.

"I made up a little poem about you," Linda said with a grin. "Would you like to hear it?"

"No, I wouldn't!" Elaine shot back, but Linda recited it anyway.

"Elly, Elly,
What a pain in the belly!
She's the janitor's kid,
That's why she's so smelly."

One or two children who were standing nearby laughed and Linda giggled loudly. Her laughter was abruptly cut short when Elaine lost her temper and flew at her.

She'd already hit Linda on the shoulder and kicked her hard on the leg, before Linda's screams brought Mr. Russell, who was on recess duty, hurrying over to them.

"Linda! Elaine! What on earth's going on?"

Neither one said anything. They looked angrily at each other.

"Linda, tell me what happened!" demanded Mr. Russell.

"Elaine hit me," Linda said, tears running down her cheeks.

"It's her fault!" Elaine said furiously. "She said something horrible about me. She's always on my back, she never leaves me alone. I'm fed up with it! I hate it here. I hate this school." She was beside herself with rage. She didn't care anymore what she did or what she said.

"Linda, go and wash your face, and sit down till the end of recess," Mr. Russell ordered. "Elaine, go and sit in the classroom."

"But I've got to find Ben," she said. "I've got to talk to him."

"It'll have to wait till lunchtime," Mr. Russell said drily. "And if you can't control your temper, you'll find yourself staying in all lunchtime too. Get going, both of you."

Elaine sat in the classroom, but it did not help her calm down. If anything, it made her feel worse. Sitting still was always the hardest thing for her to do. If she had been able to work out some of her anxiety on the monkey bars or on the grass, she might have been able to regain her self-control. Instead her rage grew and grew.

At the end of the morning, when the other students had left the classroom, Mr. Russell called her over.

"Stay put a moment, Elaine."

"But I've got to talk to Ben," she protested.

"He's not going to disappear. This will only take a few minutes."

She sighed in exasperation and stood in front of his desk, her face mutinous, her eyes lowered.

Mr. Russell sat on his desk so that their faces were more or less level. "I'm trying to help you," he said. "I'm trying to give you opportunities to settle in here and make the most of your talents. You've got a lot of them. But you're not helping me, and you're not helping yourself. Do you know what I'm talking about?"

When she didn't say anything, he said firmly, but still kindly, "I'm waiting for an answer from you, Elaine. Look at me and speak to me."

She looked at him then. Her eyes were furious. "There's no point trying to help me," she shouted. "There's no point in any of it! And don't bother about the gym class. I'm not going to be here next term. Dad wants to leave town."

"And you don't want to go?" he said calmly. "Is that what's wrong?"

"That and other things." Elaine flinched slightly, and an unreasoning panic began to flood through her. She twisted around.

Mr. Russell followed her gaze. "What are you looking at?" he said.

"Nothing!" she said, forcing her eyes away. "Oh, what's

the point of talking about it," she went on bitterly. "You can't do anything to help. Nobody can."

He looked at her in concern, his eyebrows raised, his mouth curved in a sympathetic smile. "I might be able to help more than you think. I'll have a talk with your father when he comes up to the school this afternoon."

That won't do much good, Elaine thought to herself. You don't know Dad. He won't even listen. She wanted to get away. "Can I go now?" she asked. Her panic made her sound rude.

Mr. Russell sighed and stood up. "Yes, go and get your lunch. Maybe it will improve your mood!"

It was only then that she remembered that she hadn't brought any lunch. And she hadn't had any breakfast either. No wonder I feel so strange, she thought. I feel as though I'm fading away. I probably am! Maybe Ben will let me share his sandwich.

As she came out of the classroom, she could see Ben sitting on the far side of the playground. She ran across to him. He was looking straight at her, but he didn't smile or wave. He gave absolutely no sign of recognition. She slowed down, unaccountably stricken. What had happened? Didn't he like her anymore? Had he seen her fighting with Linda?

Worse was to come. Now his eyes focused on where she was, but instead of recognition a look of horror crossed his face. He jumped up, his sandwich fell from his hand, and his lunchbox tipped over, spilling its contents on the bench before falling onto the ground. He backed away from her.

"No!" he said in a strangled voice. "No!"

"Ben," she called, standing still. Her rage seemed to drain away. All that mattered was that he didn't seem to like her anymore—he didn't even appear to know her. She was no longer angry. She felt quite empty inside, as though she no longer had any feelings.

Ben's face was returning to normal, but there was still fear in his eyes. "Elly!" he said loudly. He walked up to her and touched her arm. The gesture reassured her. She almost felt able to smile.

"What's going on?" Ben said.

"Why?" she answered. "What's wrong?"

"Elly, I didn't see you just then. I didn't see you at all until you spoke. I thought you were a space demon!"

They stared at each other. Elaine began to shake. "I'm not, am I?" she asked, terrified. "What do I look like now?"

"You look like yourself again now. Only . . ."

"Only what?"

"You look as if you might fade away any minute!"

"It's all Andrew's fault," she said wretchedly. "He's let those things out of the game, and now they're trying to take us over. Oh, I hate him. I hate him!"

"Stop it!" Ben cried. "You're going again!" He held her arm tightly. "Don't hate him! That's what's doing it!"

With a huge effort she stopped herself from thinking about Andrew. She concentrated instead on the boy beside her. She looked at his thin ordinary face and thought how kind it was. He looked back at her intently. After a few moments he sighed, let go of her, and stepped back. "That's better," he said. "Do you feel okay now?"

"I'm terribly hungry," she said. She was trembling all over.

"Don't you have any lunch?" Ben retrieved his sandwich. "Here," he said, brushing it off and breaking it in half, "have some of this. It's a Challis special—cheese, pickles, lettuce, tomato, and mayonnaise!"

After the sandwich they had half a granola bar and half an apple each. Elaine was thinking how lucky she was to have someone who would share his lunch with her. She wasn't sure if it was that or the food itself that was making her feel better. By the time they had finished eating, she was beginning to feel more like her ordinary self again.

"How do I look now?" she asked. Ben studied her closely. "Better," he said. "Definitely less transparent." He turned his head carefully, looking behind him. "Just checking on those dark shapes," he whispered. "How much can you see?"

Elaine moved her head cautiously. The shadows flicked away on the edge of her vision. "They're still there," she said nervously.

"They're getting bigger," Ben said. "I'm sure they're trying to take us over." He looked down at his lunchbox, which was still lying on the ground, and kicked it suddenly and fiercely. "I thought I could stay out of the whole thing," he said angrily. "I didn't want anything to do with it. But now that things have gotten so serious, I'm going to *have* to do something. I'll have to go up to Andrew's after school and see what's going on."

Elaine said, "But . . . where is Andrew?"

"Oh, he's all right . . . well, so far, anyway," Ben replied. "He had to go to the doctor—I asked Mr. Russell at recess. I'm more worried about Mario Ferrone." He looked at Elaine. "John told you he didn't come home last night?" Elaine nodded. Ben went on, "Well, if he's where I think he is, he's in desperate need of help. And then there's us. We're in danger too. The space demons could take us over at any moment." He studied her face briefly, then went on awkwardly, "Elaine, are you in some kind of trouble?"

She felt herself get red. "Why?"

"You looked kind of fed up when you got to school, and then you had that blow-up with Linda. . . ."

"She's such a creep," Elaine said hotly. "Did you hear that awful poem she made up about me?" Thinking about it made her start to boil again.

"Watch it!" Ben cried. "Don't get angry! That's what's making you fade away. That's how the whole thing works—that's how the game's programmed. It's responding to hate."

"How can I help it?" Elaine said desperately. "I'm having the worst time I've ever had in my life. Linda's horrible to me, Mr. Russell doesn't like me anymore, Dad's taking me away, and Andrew's space demons are after me. What am I supposed to do? Just smile at them all and say, 'That's okay, folks, trample all over me, I love you anyway'? I can't do that! No way!"

Ben surprised her by jumping suddenly to his feet. "Come on!" he said. "We need to *do* something. Come and show me how to do that double somersault on the bars. And we've got to start planning that show Mr. Russell wants us to put on. Let's talk about that too."

He had acted on an impulse, but it worked. By the time the bell rang again, Elaine had recovered some of her cheerfulness and self-confidence. Looking at her Ben thought she would probably make it through the afternoon. And then, he thought with a shiver, then I'll go over to Andrew's and do whatever needs to be done.

As they went toward the classroom, Elaine said to him, "Wait for me after school! I'm coming with you."

18

Andrew sat in front of the computer. The vortex swirled before his eyes, and in his hand he held a new gun from the game. He gazed numbly at it. He had done it! He had played through all the stages, been in and out of the game so many times he had lost count, and finally he had built up a high enough score to bring out the second gun. It had been desperately difficult, but he felt no real sense of elation or pride, only a flicker of grim satisfaction at having outwitted the program. He could still hear its voice echoing in his head. "Congratulations!" it had said sarcastically, no longer courteous. "But don't think you can defeat me. I have never been defeated, and I never release what is mine." He ignored it. It's probably lying anyway, he reassured himself. I've gotten this far, I can get farther. It's only a game. It's programmed to be played. I'm going to play it right to the end. And I'm going to win.

He stood up and stretched his arms over his head, exhausted. He needed something to keep him awake—something to eat and maybe a cup of coffee—and then he'd try to get into the vortex.

Thinking about it he unlocked his bedroom door and went out onto the landing. Standing there he could hear his mother's voice on the phone in her bedroom. She was talking loudly, almost shouting.

". . . he's locked himself in his room, and I can't get him to open the door . . . I think he must be playing that game. He's obsessed with it—he never stops playing it. I can hear the computer going, but I can't make him hear . . ."

Mom must have been trying to get in while I was in the game, Andrew thought. Good thing I locked the door! I'd better tell her I'm here.

As he began to push open the door to her room, he heard her say, ". . . Keith Freeman this morning. Keith thinks he's quite disturbed. He couldn't get him to talk about what's on his mind. . . . No, I haven't told him, but he must have guessed. . . . I find it very hard to talk to him about it. . . . Why don't *you* come home and tell him?" This last sentence was said with such anger that Andrew was astonished. Suddenly feeling that he shouldn't be listening to this conversation, he walked quietly away and down the stairs. She must have been talking to Dad, he thought. She's phoning him to talk about me. She thinks I'm cracking up. And Dr. Freeman thinks I'm disturbed.

These thoughts followed one another across his mind like images across a screen, and he watched them as though they had nothing to do with him. He suspected that if he linked them together, they would add up to something, but he avoided the thought. One thing at a time, he reasoned. First I'll play this game through. I'll get Mario out, then I'll deal with it, whatever it is. In the meantime I need something to eat, and then I'd better try to calm Mom down.

His mother came into the kitchen while he was making himself a sandwich. "Oh, Andrew," she said with relief. "How're you feeling now?"

"Much better," he said cheerfully, giving her a dazzling smile. "Those pills must be great!" He was pleased with this comment. It wasn't really a lie, he thought, they probably are great, even if I didn't take them!

"Did you take a nap?"

"Well, I was pretty tired," he said, choosing the words

carefully. He put the sandwich on a plate. The kettle was boiling, and he poured the boiling water into a mug with instant coffee.

"Do you want some, Mom?"

"Yes, that would be nice," she replied. She smiled and sat down. Andrew made her cup of coffee with great care and gave it to her with a flourish.

"Thank you," she said, taking a sip. "That's just how I like it."

They sat together in silence. Andrew tried to think of something normal to say in order to reassure his mother further, but his mind was a blank. He couldn't think of anything. He was distracted by the thudding of his own heart and by the sensation that he was still holding the gun in his right hand. He slipped his hand into his pocket, and then his fingers quickly wrapped themselves around the gun. It was a part of him. He had to follow wherever it was going to take him.

His mother was again looking at him as if she wanted to say something. Desperately, hoping to forestall her, he asked, "Is there anything on TV tonight?"

But she had evidently decided to seize the moment. "Let's check later. There's something I've got to tell you."

He had a panicky feeling. *This is it. I can't get away this time.* His heart thudded.

"What?" he said.

The front door bell rang.

Andrew jumped up with relief, saying, "I'll go answer it." His relief doubled when he opened the door and saw who it was.

"Ben!" he said. "Hello, Elaine. This is fantastic! How did you know I needed to see you?"

"We figured," Ben said. "What on earth's going on?"

"Like where's Mario?" Elaine said.

Andrew took a quick look back into the house to see if his mother could hear them. "Don't talk about that here," he said. "Come on in. We'll go upstairs. I'll tell you everything. And then I think I'm going to need your help."

"Mom," he shouted down the hallway. "Ben and Elaine are here. We're just going upstairs for a minute."

"All right," she said, coming to the kitchen door. She leaned against the door frame and sighed. As Andrew ran up the stairs, she called to him, "You'd better take another couple of pills, Andrew. You're supposed to take two every four hours."

"Okay," he shouted back. He took two pills out of the bottle on his bedside table and solemnly placed them under the pillow with the others. He looked at Ben and grinned. "They're great," he said. "They're making a huge difference in my behavior."

"What's wrong with you?" Ben asked curiously.

"I'm very disturbed. That's what Dr. Keith Freeman, your friendly neighborhood psychiatrist, thinks!"

"You went to a psychiatrist?"

"Yeah, Mom thinks I'm going crazy." Then he grew more serious and said, "You can't blame her. She doesn't know anything about the space demons. And ever since I've started playing the game I've been doing some pretty weird things. It seems to affect you like that."

"You can say that again," Elaine said. "It's affecting me very badly."

When Andrew looked at her, Ben said quietly, "She nearly turned into a space demon this afternoon. They're getting bigger—more and more real. The demons feed on hate. The angrier you are—the more you hate people— the bigger they grow."

"I know," Andrew said. "You have to *not* hate them instead. That keeps them away. That's what I've been doing all afternoon."

It was something Elaine had been finding very hard to do. Since lunchtime she had been holding the demons at bay by an act of will, and by now she was very tired. Andrew was annoying her immensely: He looked so smug and complacent here in his luxurious house, and she thought he was acting as if it was not all his fault, which it was. He had no right to be looking so pleased with himself!

"What did you do to Mario?" she said accusingly.

In the room reality began to alter slightly.

"Watch it, Elaine," Ben warned.

Andrew said evenly, "He was hit by a demon on the cliff face. Okay—it *was* my fault. He thought I was covering for him—and I wasn't."

"Just a mistake, right?" Ben asked.

Andrew shook his head. "No, I did it deliberately. He did something despicable to me, and I wanted to pay him back."

"You rat!" Elaine burst out. "Just the sort of thing you would do!"

"Probably," Andrew said, his voice calm. He went on talking to Ben. "Now I'm trying to get back into the game to find out what's happened to him. I played through all the stages this afternoon and I got another gun. Look." He took it out of his pocket and showed it to him.

Elaine did not feel like being ignored. "Aren't you

brilliant!" she sneered. "Do you want us all to clap now or later?"

"Elly," Ben begged. "Cool it! You're not helping!"

He was aware of a presence in the room, growing more noticeable and more insistent, but Elaine did not notice it—or if she did, she was too angry to care. "You are the most arrogant person I have ever met," she said to Andrew. She was aware that something was going to go wrong, but she was glad. She hoped it would hurt him, teach him a lesson. She cast around in her mind for the worst thing she could say to him. Then she remembered what he had said to her, in that very room—the hurtful, hateful words he had thrown at her that had made her want to kill him. Now she could pay him back.

"I'm not surprised your father ran off," she said triumphantly. "Who'd want to stay around with a spoiled, conceited brat like you!"

Ben realized that several things were happening all at once with incredible speed. He saw a space demon materialize right behind Elaine. He saw her begin to fade into it. At the same moment he heard Andrew gasp in anger and shock, and he heard the gun flash. The vortex began to scream. Elaine, her face white and furious, was whirled and dragged around. She opened her mouth, but before she could speak, she was pulled into the screen.

The room was full of black shapes. Ben gave a low cry of fear and began to back away toward the door. Andrew spoke to him in an urgent tone, "Don't be scared of them. They've got to obey the rules of the game." His eyes were half closed and he was concentrating desperately on something inside himself. "Hold your mind steady, Ben," he said. "They have to fade."

And they did. Ben turned his head tentatively. The dark shapes swung away behind him. They were still there, but they were no longer real enough to break into his dimension. He let out his breath in a sigh. Andrew opened his eyes. They both looked at the screen.

For several moments Elaine was clearly visible. They watched her float over the cliff face and disappear into one of the tunnels.

"You shot her," Ben whispered in outrage. "You sent her back into the game again!"

"I *know!*" Andrew hissed, trying to control his feelings. "She got under my skin—just for a moment. I was trying not to let her, but I couldn't help it. She drove me to it, her and the demons. I wanted to hurt her—and that was it!" He rested his head on his hands for a few moments, looking desperately at the screen. "At least she's still herself," he said. "That's one thing. She hasn't changed into a space demon. I thought she was going. I thought she'd had it!"

The *wheeee* and *tktktktktk* sounds began to echo through the room.

"Here comes the first demon," he said.

Ben stared at the screen. "But that's not a demon," he whispered. "Isn't it Mario?"

The tiny figure was instantly recognizable. It was Mario, scaling the cliff, gun in hand. Then, to the boys' astonishment, another Mario, identical to the first, began to cross the cliff horizontally. *Wheeee—tktktktktk*—went the computer, and more and more of the tiny figures, like hideous clones, advanced through the game.

Andrew leaned forward and banged his head on the keyboard. "Oh, no!" he groaned. "I see what's happened! When Mario was shot by the demons, he became one. The game is using him as a pattern for making demons, using his energy to create more of them. It's horrible!"

"There *must* be some way we can get him out!" Ben cried.

"Even if I got back into the game," Andrew said grimly, "the only way I can get out again is by shooting demons, and that would mean I'd have to shoot him—shoot Mario—over and over again. And what would that do to him? No, it's got us this time, it's got us in a corner. It's won." He paced up and down the room, thinking frantically. The gun weighed heavy in his hand, his head ached, and he was bone weary. He thought longingly of the pills under his pillow. If only he could take the whole batch and slide off into oblivion, leaving this nightmarish situation he had created behind him.

"I told you it was dangerous," Ben said bitterly. "Why didn't you stop when I told you to? It's all your fault, Andrew!"

"I know it's my fault," Andrew said. "There's no need to rub it in."

He forced himself to think back over all the stages of the game, trying to remember some weakness in it, some point where he could outthink it; but he kept coming back to the same conclusion—the only thing to do was to play on. And the only way to do that was to get back into the game. And the only way to do that was to . . .

He looked at the gun, made a face of resignation, and held it against his stomach.

"What are you doing?" Ben asked.

"I'm going to get back into the game," Andrew replied calmly. "I think I can do it now. You've got to really loathe yourself to get yourself in. I was never able to do it before. But I think I know myself a bit better now."

"But what am *I* going to do?" Ben said in alarm. "What

if none of you ever comes back? What am I going to say?"

Andrew turned to Ben with one of his familiar confident grins. "Don't worry," he said. "We'll get out. I'm going to win! It's all in the program!"

Then his face tightened as he began the painful task of looking clearly and squarely at himself.

The game had trapped him in the first place because he had been vain and conceited. It had flattered him and he had believed the flattery, thinking it to be only the truth. Then he had used others—first Ben, then Elaine, and finally Mario—used them against their will, just so he could continue playing the game. He had said terrible things to them and had done terrible things to them. Each of them had called him conceited, spoiled, and stuck-up —and each of them was right. He groaned as he saw with piercing lucidity how right they were. There was a brief, agonizing moment when he could not bear to look at himself any longer.

It was enough. The gun flashed. Ben, watching, saw Andrew's expression of pain give way to one of triumph as he was pulled through the screen. The noise of the vortex seemed louder than ever. Ben covered his ears with his hands, but his eyes were on Andrew as the tiny figure plunged downward. Shots began to blast across the screen almost immediately, as the Mario-demons became aware of Andrew's entry back into the game. Ben watched in terror. Andrew was not firing back. Instead the little figure dodged the attack until the cliff solidified and the tunnels appeared, and then dived swiftly into one of them. But before vanishing completely from sight, he turned back and gave a distinct thumbs-up gesture.

Ben could not help thinking, Typical Andrew! He wished he shared his confidence.

19

It had been an act of bravado, not one of confidence. As he dived for the safety of the tunnels, Andrew had no idea what he was going to do. True, he had made it back into the game, but he was powerless. He did not want to use the gun again—but what other options were there?

There must be some way out, he thought to himself. Games are made to be played. They are designed to be won. No one makes a game that can't be won. I just have to find out what to do next.

He listened for the voice of the program; perhaps it would give him some clues. But it was silent. He could hear only the electronic pulse going *thud thud thud* through him and the game in unison, and the menacing sounds of the Mario-demons as they crossed the cliff face beyond where he hid. He looked back at the circle of light through which he had plunged into the game, and then he went forward into the tunnel.

He had to grit his teeth and clench his fists to make himself do it. His whole being cried out against piercing that utter darkness where once before he had waited for Mario, desperate and afraid. It was no longer thrilling, the way it had been the first time—so long ago it seemed now—when he had been sent hurtling through the screen by Elaine.

Elaine! He wondered where she was. Then he remembered the words she had said to him, the words that had made him lash out at her and want to kill her. They puzzled him. Why had she said them? They weren't true. His father had not left home. He was just away in the city working . . . wasn't he?

His fear was compounded by something else. He started to tremble. Suddenly everything within his head became brilliantly clear, as though someone had just switched on a thousand-watt spotlight. All the half-understood sentences he had overheard, all the puzzling things that people had been saying to him—his mother, Mr. Russell, Dr. Freeman—all fell into place.

It's true. Dad has left home. My parents have separated.

He gave a cry of outrage and pain. How could they do this to him? What an idiot they were making of him! The fact that they could get to a point where they could decide to separate, without telling him about it or giving him any warning, made him feel as if they had reduced him to a zero. He was furious with them. He felt the power of the gun in his hand. He wanted revenge. He wanted to kill.

"The hell with it!" he raged. "I'm going back to the cliff face and wipe out every one of those demon figures— Mario or not. If I can't win, I'm going to take as many with me as I can."

Excellent! said a suave, cool voice in his mind. *You will then get out of the game. When you have killed enough of them, you will reach the cliff top. Good luck,* it added encouragingly. *It's a pleasure to deal with a champion.*

It's flattering me again, Andrew thought with dislike. I don't trust it. The voice of the program, praising and encouraging him, made him stop and think. His rage cooled a little. I mustn't get so angry, he thought. The angrier I am, the more likely I am to make a mistake, and the more I come under the program's power. And then it controls me until I'm not thinking for myself anymore.

He breathed slowly and deeply to calm himself. Something in his chest seemed to be trying to climb up his throat and choke him. He was glad it was dark because the same something was also trying to burst out through his eyes, and it was making them water dreadfully. He made a strangled noise that sounded like a sob.

The voice spoke with contempt. *Are you ready to give up? There is no way you can win. You will never beat me.*

"No," he said aloud. "I am not ready to give up. You said the game has to be played to the end, and that's what I'm going to do."

He heard his own voice echoing away down the tunnels. Through the echoes the program spoke again. *The end is very bitter,* it said, mock-apologetically.

Andrew did not bother to answer. Resolve was forming inside him. He put away his rage and his grief and tried not to think about what had caused them. "I'll deal with that later," he said to himself.

He pressed on through the darkness. I might find Elaine, he thought. Perhaps she knows something I don't know. And then at least I won't be alone.

Elaine was sitting in the dark feeling more like a fool than she had ever felt in her life. It was not a comfortable feeling. "How could I have been so dumb?" she questioned herself over and over again. "Why on earth didn't I listen to Ben? I knew what was going to happen—and it nearly did!"

She shivered as she thought of the dreadful moment when she had felt the darkness of the demon starting to take her over. The blast of hate from Andrew, painful as it was, had almost been a relief. At last it had swept her away from the dark force that was overpowering her.

At any rate, I hope it did, she thought, trembling. There's no way I can tell in here. It's too dark to see anything. What if I've changed into one of those creatures and I don't know it?

She tried to make out her hand in front of her, but it remained invisible in the total blackness. Perhaps I'm blind, she thought to herself in panic. Perhaps everything's come to an end and there's going to be nothing but this blackness forever and ever. Perhaps I'm dead!

Then she thought, I might as well be. What a mess I made of everything! I thought I was going to Andrew's with Ben to help, and in the end I just made things worse! I wonder what they're doing now? I wonder if anyone's going to come in after me.

She did not think they would be able to. She was not familiar enough with the game, but she was sure that Andrew could not send himself in. And Ben had hated being in the game before. He would never come in again.

How on earth did I get into this mess? What happened to me? Where did it all start?

She looked back over the past few weeks, trying to unravel the events. They were so interwoven that it was hard to pull them apart so she could see them clearly. She found the end of a thread and patiently began to follow it.

Why did I come along with Ben?

To do something about the space demons.

Why are the space demons pursuing us?

Andrew let them out of the computer game.

What was I doing in the game?

Andrew made me go in.

How?

He asked me to come up to his house.

Why did I go?

I wanted to help Ben.

And?

I wanted to put one over on Linda.

Aha!

What's wrong with Linda?

She's spoiled. She's mean to me. I don't like her.

Ever wonder why?

She's got a mother to look after her and I don't!

That's getting a bit too close for comfort, Elaine thought.
She started again on another thread:

Why was I so nasty to Andrew?

I was mad at him.

Why?

He's so conceited. . . .

And?

He's got such a nice house!

Why haven't I got a nice house like that?

Because my father is a rolling stone, and my mother . . .

Oh, hell! she thought. Back to that again! Mom, she
thought desperately, It's your fault! You ran away from
me, and I'm never going to get over it! I might as well
stay here in the dark forever! I'm never going to make
anything of my life anyway. There are just too many things
against me. I might as well give up!

To her astonishment she heard a sound echoing through
the darkness toward her.

"No!" it said, ". . . not ready to give up . . . the game
has to be played to the end."

The voice was muffled and distorted, but she recognized
it. It's Andrew, she thought, amazed. He's in the game!

I'm not alone anymore! The thought cheered her up immensely. She put her hands up to her face and touched her skin carefully. "I am not a space demon," she said firmly to herself. "I am me, Elaine Jennifer Taylor. Maybe I'm going to be all right after all!" She began to make her way through the darkness in the direction of Andrew's voice.

It wasn't long before they bumped into each other. Elaine put out her hands to avoid falling.

"Ouch!" Andrew said.

"Andrew, is that you?"

"It was my eye," he said, rubbing it. He put out his hand tentatively. Something springy and light brushed against it. Although he couldn't see it, he could imagine how red Elaine's hair was. He grinned to himself, suddenly feeling much more cheerful.

"Hey, I've come to rescue you!" he said.

"The hell you have!" she snapped back. She couldn't help it, it just came out. "You're more likely to need *me* to rescue *you*!" She regretted her words instantly. That's no good, she thought. I've got to try and get along with Andrew. If only he wasn't always so aggravating!

"Don't be angry and don't argue," Andrew said. "It's very dangerous around here!"

"Well, let's get out then," Elaine said, controlling herself with an effort. "What do we do, the same as before? Shoot all the demons? You'd better give me a gun."

"It's more complicated this time," Andrew said. "The demons aren't demons anymore. They're Mario, and I don't know if I'm ready to shoot them!"

"Then what are we going to do?" Elaine said.

Andrew shrugged. Elaine couldn't see him in the dark,

but she knew he was shrugging because she was holding his hand. She couldn't think how that had happened. She let go of it in a hurry.

"It's all right," he said. "We can hold hands if you want to. It might help you not to feel so scared."

"I am *not* scared," she said bitingly and not entirely truthfully. "And I don't want to hold your hand. I wouldn't hold it if you were the last person on earth!"

Andrew could have pointed out that he might as well be the last person on earth, but he didn't want to make her angrier. So instead he said, as nicely as he could, "I'm sorry."

"What?"

"I said, I'm sorry. I'm sorry I sent you into the game. I'm sorry I got mad at you. I am really sorry for all the things I've said and done to you." He was grateful for the darkness then. It made these things easier to say.

Elaine was dumbfounded. "Why are you saying that?" she asked suspiciously.

"Because if we keep on being mad at each other, we'll never get out of the game. So we might as well try to get along and work something out together." He reached out and felt for her hand again. Finding it, he gave it a friendly squeeze. "See?"

She frowned, a long way from being convinced. "Are you really sorry, or are you just sorry because you want to get out of here?" All the same, she did not pull her hand away.

"I am really and truly sorry." He sounded sincere—but then Andrew always did, and she couldn't see his face.

"Let's keep holding hands, okay?" he said as they started to move along. "I don't want us to get separated. We might as well start by exploring the tunnels. We can't get out on the cliff, it's too risky." He knew the attack pattern, but Elaine did not. He had played the game dozens of times before with Mario, but she had only been in it once. There was no way she could dodge the demons on the cliff face. Their only hope was to discover something else about the game in the tunnels.

His confidence was coming and going in waves. Right now it was on the way out again. Feelings of dread and despair were trying to get a hold on him. He guessed that they were coming from the program: It was trying to sap his resolve and get him to give in, and he was finding it hard to resist.

"Elaine," he said, "do you think you could talk to me? It might help."

Elaine then decided to say what had been weighing on her mind. "I'm sorry too. I'm sorry I said that about your dad."

"It's true. They have split up." He was amazed at how calmly he could say it. "But how did you know?"

Elaine felt very uncomfortable. "Somebody at school told me."

An intense feeling of shame swept over him. "You mean everybody at school knows?"

"No, only the teachers. Actually it was Mrs. Fields who told me, and she shouldn't have. I wish she hadn't!"

When he didn't say anything, she went on. "I'm sorry I said it, but I'm sorry it's happened too. I think it's really tough."

"Oh, well," Andrew replied lightly, "that's life. It happens to a lot of people. There's not much you can do about it."

"Doesn't it bother you?" she asked, surprised.

"Yeah, it bothers me. It makes me really mad. But I'm not going to let it spoil my life. I mean, a little while ago

I thought it was going to destroy me. I thought it would finish me off. But I'm not going to let it."

Somewhere in Elaine's mind a door opened. It shut again almost immediately, but not before she had had time to glimpse a completely different way of being herself. The revelation stunned her. Her heart began to beat with excitement. "How do you stop it?"

Andrew thought for a moment. "For one thing, I'm not going to blame myself," he said. "It's not my fault—they made their decision, and they have to act on it."

"I had a fight with my dad last night," Elaine confided. "He never talks about my mom very much, but last night he said quite a lot, more than he's ever said before. He told me she never really cared for me." She, too, was amazed now at her own calmness.

"Well, she should have!" Andrew declared. "Parents are supposed to look after their children. There's nothing wrong with you. It's her problem. There's nothing wrong with me either. Just because our parents can't get it together doesn't mean we have to go to pieces too. And we're not going to turn into some sort of damaged goods either—'the product of a broken home.' I don't believe in all that crap. We're going to be okay. We're going to survive."

"If we ever get out of here," Elaine reminded him.

Never! they heard a sardonic voice intone gloatingly.

Elaine froze. "What the heck was that?"

"Don't take any notice of it," Andrew reassured her. "It's the program of the game. It's trying to get us to give up. It doesn't want us to play anymore because it knows we're going to beat it. It knows it's going to lose."

You have already lost, the voice said calmly. *There is no way you can win now.*

"Is that true?" Elaine asked in alarm.

"No, it's lying," Andrew said with a certainty he was far from feeling. "Don't listen to it!"

"If we do give up, what happens to us?" Elaine asked.

"We're not going to give up!" Andrew said firmly. "We're going to play to the end!"

If you give up, you will be returned to your own world in safety, the program assured them.

"Well, that's nice to know," Elaine said.

"You can't believe a word it says," he said stubbornly. "Besides, what about Mario? I bet he doesn't get returned, does he?"

It is regretted, the voice said coldly. *The energy is essential. He cannot be returned.*

Would anyone really miss him? Andrew found himself thinking. Would anyone care? He would just be written off as one more kid who ran away from home.

Elaine was thinking the same thing. We could easily get out of this mess now, she said to herself. All we have to do is give up. Mario's such a creep anyway. We'd be doing his family a favor. They wouldn't care. An insistent little thought kept trying to surface. John would care, it reminded her. She tried to squash it.

The voice of the program said persuasively, *Give up.*

The temptation was becoming greater and greater. If only I weren't so tired, Andrew thought. If only it wasn't so dark, if only . . . I honestly don't know if I can fight back anymore. And it's not just me, there's Elaine to think about. I got her into this and I've got to get her out again. If we give in now, at least she'll have a chance of getting out.

But inside him there was an obstinate streak that would not let him surrender. He discovered it buried underneath all the other feelings, and he latched on to it.

Give up! the voice repeated.

"Get lost!" he flung back. "Come on, Elaine!"

They moved on quickly through the darkness. To her surprise Elaine found she was lightheaded with relief. "I thought you were going to give in!" she said. "I nearly did. It was like I forgot Mario was a real person. I was just thinking he was like one of those little demons that we shot before. He could be zapped and it wouldn't matter a bit. And now I can see that it would matter a lot. Of course it would. He's a person, he's got a family that cares about him. John cares about him."

"I don't know why I didn't give in," Andrew admitted. "I was thinking all those things too. That's what this game does to you. It makes you think that nothing's very important, that people don't matter very much—they're just there to be used as part of the game. I wasn't even being very noble, or anything," he added honestly. "It's just that I can't bear to lose. But as soon as I'd said it, I remembered that in a funny sort of way I do care about Mario too. I mean, there really are things about him that I like!"

Elaine looked in the direction his voice was coming from. To her surprise she realized she could make out his face.

"Hey," she said in excitement, "it's getting lighter!"

"Be careful!" Andrew said. "That means we're getting near the surface again."

The tunnel curved up toward a circle of dazzling light. It streamed into the darkness, illuminating Elaine's red head and Andrew's blond one. From beyond the light they could hear the *tktktktk* of the guns blasting across the screen. Then a silhouette passed across the mouth of the tunnel. They could clearly see the black spiky hair and the pale face, set in a dreadful expression of anguish.

"Oh, how awful!" Elaine cried with a shudder. Andrew felt exactly the same way. There could be nothing worse than being trapped inside this evil game and being used for its purposes of terror and destruction. But before he could say or do anything, the figure turned to face them. To their horror, fiery tracers of red and orange blazed from its weapon toward them.

Their hands parted as they threw themselves violently to opposite sides of the tunnel. The shots whined between them viciously and flew off into the darkness.

The silhouetted figure passed again across the face of the tunnel and disappeared. They could hear its gun, still firing, fading away outside. But other sounds of firing were not fading away. They were getting stronger, louder . . . *closer!*

"What's happening?" Elaine cried. "Why aren't we safe in the tunnels anymore?"

"Mario can move in three dimensions like us," Andrew said miserably. "He doesn't have to keep to the two dimensions of the space demons. And now that the game's using his energy, it can send the demons it's cloning from him into the tunnels after us. We can't even hide from them anymore." He lifted the gun. "I'll have to use it," he said. "I don't see any alternative. I don't want to, but what else can we do? It's one thing not to want to wipe Mario out—but I don't think I can just stand here and let him shoot me!"

Elaine looked desperately back into the darkness. A flash of light made her gasp. "Look!" she said breathlessly. "Look!"

Andrew jumped and swung around, his gun ready, but all he saw was a faint tremor in the blackness as though something had just been wiped off it.

"You missed it," she said, a note of despair in her voice. "But I saw it. I've seen it before too. I saw it the last time I was in the game. It's a message printed across the screen. It says, TO TERMINATE GAME REPLACE GUN HERE. There we are! That's it! That's our way out! We can stop the game now just by giving back the gun!"

Outside, the noise of firing grew closer.

Andrew gripped the gun. "I'm not giving it up now," he said. "It's our only chance of getting out. Besides, it's probably a trick. You can't trust anything the program says."

Elaine reached out to take the gun from him, but when she touched it, a replica formed in her own hand instead. She gazed at it, frustrated.

Andrew smiled grimly in approval. "That's good," he said. "We'll have much more of a chance if we're both armed."

"No! No!" she cried. "That's not the way to do it! I know it's not! That's what the game's hoping you'll do. It wants you to fight. It wants you to destroy Mario completely— then it will destroy us too! It's making us fight and hate again. As long as we've got the guns, we can't stop wanting to use them on somebody!" She stared again at the replica gun and shook her head in exasperation. "I'm not keeping it," she said. "I'm putting it back where the message appeared."

She pushed herself away from Andrew and let the game's momentum carry her back down the tunnel. Then she placed the replica gun carefully back into the darkness, as if putting it away on a shelf, and turned to face Andrew. "Quick!" she said. "Do it now! Quickly!"

A shadow darkened the mouth of the tunnel. Andrew swung instinctively toward it.

"Don't shoot, Andrew!" Elaine screamed. "Put the gun back! Now!"

The figure fired at them. Andrew turned to duck the shots and found himself next to Elaine. He either had to trust her and do what she said, or he had to fire at Mario. He came to the decision in a split second. He let go of the gun. It merged perfectly and invisibly with the darkness.

Nothing else happened. The Mario-demon passed across the screen. The noises of the game continued. Everything remained the same. Immediately Andrew was convinced that they had made a fatal mistake. They had fallen for a trick.

"That's it then," he said quietly. "It's won. It fooled us."

Elaine was silent for a minute. Then she whispered, "I'm sorry, Andrew. That was my fault."

"It doesn't matter," Andrew told her. He felt strangely cheerful about it. His hand felt lighter, and his head did not pulse so much. He laughed. He felt quite carefree and happy. The worst had happened. There was nothing left to fear and nothing left to worry about.

You won! he thought inside his head to the program. Then he thought, I wonder why it's not saying anything? I would have expected it to say "I told you so," or something like that. Oh, well, I guess it's saving that up for when we're being used for making demons. Then he thought, I don't think it could make demons from me at the moment. I've never felt less demon-like!

Still it did not dawn on him what had happened. He still believed they had lost.

"Come on," he said to Elaine. "Let's go out and face them. If we're going to go, let's go out in the light."

Elaine took his hand. She, too, felt surprisingly happy. When she had put back the gun, she'd had the feeling she was giving up something else as well, something she'd been carrying around for a long time. Without it she felt free.

The shots across the screen continued relentlessly. Now another dark figure appeared across the mouth of the tunnel, gun in hand, face twisted and hate-filled.

Poor Mario, Andrew thought, and without even meaning to, he called out, "Mars, it's not your fault. I got you into this. And I'm sorry."

The gun did not fire. The light around the black shape grew more dazzling, like the sun emerging from behind the moon's shadow after an eclipse. The shape itself became less and less dense. It was growing transparent. Now they could see light through it quite clearly. As they watched in amazement, it faded away altogether. Andrew glided to the lip of the tunnel and looked out across the cliff face. A number of tiny Marios were crossing it from every direction. He jumped back into the tunnel as tracers flashed past him.

Then he put his head out again and called to the nearest figure, "Mars, you're the greatest! You're a champion demon hunter!"

The little figure was absorbed into the light. Andrew laughed gleefully.

"What's happening?" Elaine asked. "What's going on?"

Andrew ducked back next to her. "You know what a great guy Mario is?" he said. "You know how much everybody admires him?"

She looked at him silently, not understanding.

"You know all the great things he can do—he's so brave, and so cool, and so . . . help, I've run out," he said.

"He stands up for himself, and he doesn't let anyone boss him around," Elaine said.

"Yeah, yeah, that's right. Better think of some more.

We're going to need dozens!" Andrew was giggling helplessly.

"What *are* you talking about, Andrew?" Elaine was afraid he'd gone mad.

"What am I talking about? We're going to make it, that's what I'm talking about! Everything nice we can think about Mars is lethal to those little demons out there. We've discovered the ultimate demonicide! You were right—the program wasn't tricking us. We've won, Elaine! We've won!"

20

Ben looked anxiously from the computer screen to the window. Darkness was falling. It was getting late. He should have been at home, but he could not leave before he found out what had happened to Andrew and Elaine. He could see nothing of them on the screen of the computer. The only thing he could see were the seemingly endless tiny copies of Mario that crossed the cliff face, shooting their miniature dark weapons in a lethal barrage.

They'll never get out of the tunnels, Ben thought. There's nothing they can do! He watched in agony, not knowing which would be worse—to see a battle begin between Andrew and the Mario-demons, or to wait endlessly for nothing else to happen at all. He tried not to think about either alternative: He had no idea what he would do or how he would explain what had happened to anyone else. Along with all his other fears, easily the greatest at the moment was his fear that Andrew's mother might suddenly come into the room and ask him where Andrew was. She usually came up at about this time to tell him it was time to go home. What on earth would he say to her then?

I could just *go* home, he thought desperately. If I go now, I could call out good-bye to her and she would think Elaine was with me, and she wouldn't know Andrew wasn't still here. But, tempting though the idea was, he somehow could not tear himself away from the computer.

Then there were the space demons. They were hanging around behind him. He was aware they were waiting for something. What would happen to him if Elaine and Andrew lost? Would he, too, disappear into the game, absorbed by the space demons? Would all four of them simply disappear forever? Oh, Andrew, he thought angrily. Why did you get us all into this?

The demons grew more menacing. Terrified, he swallowed hard. That was what they did: They latched onto any feeling you had of anger or hate, and then they used it to make you more afraid. He tried to hold his mind steady. They had to obey the rules of the game, Andrew had told him. Ben tried to believe that. He put away the anger. The thought came to him that perhaps in some way he was actually helping the others in the game, perhaps he was weakening the program's evil power by refusing to hate. He put his whole concentration behind it. The oppression lifted slightly, and he began to breathe more easily.

Then he heard a sound that set his heart pounding and his breathing racing again. Someone was coming up the stairs! He looked feverishly around the room for a place to hide, but there was no time. The door was already opening. As Andrew's mother came in, he flung himself down in the chair in front of the computer and pretended to be absorbed in the game.

She stopped short in surprise when she saw that Ben was the only person in the room.

"Hi, Mrs. Hayford," he said without turning around, peering into the screen as if he was at a crucial stage. His heart was pounding so fiercely he could hardly speak.

"Did Andrew go out and leave you on your own?" she inquired.

"Yeah," Ben said. "That's right."

"Oh," she said. There was a pause. "Where did he go?"

"He and, um, and Elaine . . . went off somewhere," Ben said desperately.

Andrew's mother frowned. "That's funny! I didn't hear them come downstairs. Are you sure?"

Ben didn't answer, for he couldn't think of anything at all to say. Mrs. Hayford sighed. "Really!" she said. "You boys are all the same! Once you get started on that computer, it's like talking to a brick wall." She walked rapidly over to the monitor and reached toward the "Off" switch. Ben threw himself over the keyboard. "Please don't turn it off!" he said. "I'm . . . I'm in the middle of a terribly important game!"

She clicked her tongue in exasperation. "Well, all right, you can just finish this game, and then you have to head home. It's after six o'clock, Ben. You'll be late for dinner." She crossed over to the window to pull down the blinds. Then she turned and said to Ben, "They didn't go out on the roof, did they?"

"Uh-uh," said Ben, shaking his head and keeping his face hidden from her. He had no idea how this conversation was going to end or how he was going to get out of the room—or even *if* he was going to be able to get out of the room. If he walked out now, wouldn't Andrew's mother automatically turn off the computer? She would, he knew she would. Grown-ups had a mania for turning things off—lights, radios, televisions. He couldn't begin to think what would happen to the others then. He had to stop it from happening. He had to stay where he was and guard the game until Andrew, Elaine, and Mario returned.

From behind him Andrew's mother said, "What game are you playing?"

"It's the one called Space Demons," Ben replied. "It's very exciting," he added, thinking to himself, And that's the understatement of the year!

"Andrew's father brought it back from Japan. He said it was rather special."

"It is!" Ben agreed. "Very special!"

There was silence for a few moments. Ben wished fervently she would go out of the room and leave him alone. He was feeling more and more uncomfortable. He peered into the screen, frowning, and what he saw made him stiffen in alarm. He could still hear the sound of gun fire from the Mario figures, but he could no longer see the flashes racing across the screen. Immediately he realized why. The figures were firing only when they came to the black entrances of the tunnels, and they were firing down into them. He couldn't see the shots because they were disappearing into the darkness—the darkness where Andrew and Elaine were hiding. They were no longer safe there. They were no longer safe anywhere.

He could not think what to do. He couldn't get into the game, for the controls no longer answered to the external player. He didn't dare switch off the computer. He could only watch and wait helplessly. It was agonizing. He couldn't help groaning aloud.

"What's up?" Mrs. Hayford said. "Did you get killed?"

"Oh, no, no!" he said, thinking that would be almost preferable. "It's just a little tricky, that's all!"

"Andrew's been playing it a lot," she told him. "He really loves it." She paused and then continued, "Ben, do you think he's been all right lately?"

"Who, Andrew?" said Ben, trying to sound vague. "Oh, sure, he's been okay." She was standing right behind him now. He was terrified she would take a closer look at the game. Suppose she recognized Mario! She must certainly know what he looked like by now.

"You see, Andrew's father and I have decided to live apart for a while," Mrs. Hayford was saying. "I'm afraid that Andrew's very upset about it."

Ben heard what she was saying, but he couldn't respond, because at that moment he saw one of the Mario-demons at a tunnel entrance on the lower right of the screen disappear. It seemed to have been absorbed suddenly into a blaze of light. As he watched in astonishment, he was even more amazed to see Andrew emerge from the tunnel's mouth. He couldn't believe Mrs. Hayford wouldn't spot him: Tiny as the figure was, it was so unmistakably Andrew! Then it disappeared back into the darkness, and the nearest demon was instantly absorbed into light.

Ben gasped, "What *is* going on?" before he realized that this was not a very appropriate answer to what Andrew's mother had said to him. One part of him was feeling really sorry and angry on Andrew's behalf, while the rest of him was blazing into life with this new development in the game.

He tried to respond. "That's tough!" he said, but the

words came out too lightly, as though he didn't really care at all.

Mrs. Hayford looked at him coldly. "Just how much longer are you going to be?" she asked.

Ben felt penitent. She probably thinks it's one more example of modern technology turning kids into zombies with no feelings, he thought. He was trying to think of something more sympathetic to say, something that would stop her from ordering him out of the house, when through the noise of the game he heard a different sound. Someone was ringing the front doorbell loudly and insistently.

"That might be Andrew now," Mrs. Hayford said with a sigh of relief. She left the room.

Ben sighed, too, but his relief was mingled with excitement. He turned his head carefully. The black shapes had thinned and faded to hairline cracks again. He felt relief and happiness surge within him. "You're on your way out!" he said to them exultantly. "The game's ending! I don't know what Andrew's done, but he's done it! He's winning!"

On the screen another tiny figure blazed into light and vanished.

As the demons disappeared, the noise of the game diminished more and more. Finally it was silent. In the half-light of the tunnel's entrance Andrew and Elaine looked at each other.

"They're all gone!" Andrew said. He was laughing, intoxicated with success.

"Then why are we still here?" Elaine asked. "Shouldn't that bring us to the top of the cliff?"

Puzzled and slightly subdued, they looked out of the tunnel. One last figure was coming across the cliff. They could see that it held a gun in its hand, but it was not firing.

"Just one to go," Andrew said. He called out to it, "Hey, Mars, you're the greatest."

The figure did not blaze. It did not disappear. It simply continued toward them. As it came closer and closer, Elaine said loudly, "Mario, I really admire you! I love your hairstyle, Mars, I really do!"

Both of them backed away as the figure swung into the tunnel.

"Thanks for the appreciation!" Mario said sarcastically. "You two make quite a fan club! Now you can tell me what the hell's going on!"

Andrew put out his hand and touched him. Mario felt solid and three-dimensional and real. "Are you okay?" he asked.

"No, I am definitely not okay! I've been taken apart and put back together again about fifty thousand times! I feel lousy!" He raised the gun threateningly. "And I've got a sneaking feeling I've got you to blame for it, you little creep! You let me down back there, didn't you? You did it deliberately. You let me get shot. Well, now you can see what it feels like. It's your turn."

"Wait," Andrew said urgently. "It was my fault, it's true." He felt no anger or hatred anymore. "Like I said, I am really sorry. You can get me back if you want to. But let's get out of the game first. We've nearly got it beat. We can win if we go on now. But if you shoot me, we'll have lost."

Elaine said quietly, "You have to put the gun back, Mario."

Mario gripped it more tightly. "I'm not going to give it up," he said. "It's too important. It makes me feel powerful. It's made me feel like somebody for once in my life."

The voice of the program, which had been silent for a long time, suddenly spoke again. *I think that makes it even,* it said infuriatingly.

More like stalemate, Andrew thought. His elation and excitement were rapidly draining away. He could not believe that they were going to be cheated of victory now that they had come so close. He racked his brain to think what to do next. He could grab at the gun, and as soon as the replica formed in his hand, he could shoot Mario with it. Mario would count as the last demon, the game would end, and he and Elaine would get out—but the risk of Mario shooting him first was too great, and besides, they would not then have defeated the program. They would still have left Mario behind.

He said quickly, "We can go on hating each other and stay in here forever. Or we can cooperate and beat the system and get out. I really meant the things I said to you. They wouldn't have worked if I hadn't. There are loads of things I like about you. And I've never met anyone who's better at video games."

The gun wavered a little. Mario said, in a voice that was marginally less pugnacious, "You mean that?"

Elaine thought, He's like a stray animal. We can't hurry him. We have to take it very, very slow. She put out a hand and ran it over his black short-cropped hair. It felt thick and soft, like an animal's fur. "Neat," she said, "I really like it. Where'd you get it done? I want to have my hair cut."

"I might show you the place if we get out of here," Mario said. Andrew felt the tension beginning to ease momentarily.

"Thanks," Elaine said. With daring, she let her hand find Mario's and take it. He pulled his own away abruptly. "I can't do it," he said in a strangled voice. "I can't stop hating you and I can't give up the gun. It's too freaking dangerous. I feel safe like this."

"Safe!" Elaine exclaimed. "Safe for what? Safe for just sitting in the dark feeding this dumb game? Give it up, Mars. Otherwise it'll just keep you here in the dark forever."

"That's what it wants," Andrew said. "You want to beat it, don't you? Like I said, you're a great player, a champion. Well, the only way to win this game is by putting the gun back. If you hang onto it, the game's going to win. And you'll have lost. *Lost!*"

Mario said nothing. He looked from Andrew to Elaine and back again.

"Come on," urged Elaine. She took his hand again, and this time Mario did not pull away. He allowed her to lead him through the tunnel. Andrew followed behind them.

It was dark and totally silent. The whole world seemed to have gone on hold as it waited for the outcome. Everything now hung on Mario. It had to be his decision: No one else could do it for him. He had to let go and put the gun back—or they all had to accept defeat and remain forever in the darkness.

They had come to the message place.

In front of them the words printed rapidly and silently

across the screen: TO TERMINATE GAME REPLACE GUN HERE: TO TERMINATE GAME REPLACE GUN HERE.

Mario said, "How do I know it's for real?"

"You have to trust us," Elaine said calmly. "We're not lying to you. We like you. You should know that by now, we've told you enough times!"

"Yeah, and every time you told me, it hurt like hell!" Mario said. "It felt like someone was putting me back together with a welding tool!"

"I know that," Andrew said. He was remembering how painful his refusal to hate had been. "We went through it too. Not quite the same as you, but sort of. It kills, it really does. But it's the only thing that works!"

"I feel like I'm being sawed in half—slowly!" Mario said.

"Speed it up some!" Elaine ordered. "Put the gun back! Get it over with fast!"

Mario laughed. "You're all right!" he said. "You've got guts. I like you!"

It was easier to say things like this in the dark. Andrew had discovered that before, and now he guessed that Mario was feeling the same.

"You're not so bad yourself," Elaine said. "In fact, you're nowhere near as bad as you think you are!" To herself she said, That's what it is! It's what we think we are that makes us what we are. But changing the way you think is so painful.

With a sudden movement Mario came to his decision.

He thrust his hand forward, opened it, and let go of the gun. It merged into the blackness. Mario gave a howl of pain, as if he really were being sawed in two. Elaine grabbed him tightly, shivers running down her back, and Andrew clutched his arm from the other side. The cry of pain filled the darkness, making it even darker and more dense. It sounded like the scream of the vortex. And now, like the vortex, everything began to whirl. The three of them lost all sense of time and place as a terrible vertigo overwhelmed them. The game was being spun to pieces. The darkness and density grew and grew until there was no space for anything else in the world. While the starry sky appeared and disappeared, they were pushed to the edge and spun and squeezed until there was a moment of total blackness, a moment of endless falling . . . and one after another, still clutching each other, they tumbled through the screen, knocked Ben sideways off the chair, and fell in a heap on the thick white carpet of Andrew's room.

The screen had gone blank. Then a message began to print itself out across it: CONGRATULATIONS! YOU HAVE SUCCESSFULLY COMPLETED THE HYPERGAME SPACE DEMONS! THIS GAME IS PROGRAMMED TO ERASE ITSELF WHEN MASTERED. TO PLAY THE NEXT GAME IN THE SERIES, RETURN THE BLANK DISKETTE OF SPACE DEMONS TO THIS ADDRESS: ITO, BOX 4321, OSAKA, JAPAN.

From where they sat on the floor, the four stared at it. With an impatient flicker the screen wiped itself clean and then printed the message out again.

"Quick!" Mario said, jumping to his feet and wiping the back of his hand across his eyes. "Write it down!"

Andrew had already crawled across to his desk drawer to take out a pencil and a piece of paper. He was writing down the address.

"What do you think you're doing?" Ben demanded. "You're not going to send for it, are you?"

"Sure he is!" Mario said, his eyes bright, his face alight with excitement.

"Well, I might not," Andrew said. His eyes were gleaming too. "But I want to have the address just in case!"

The letters were already fading from the screen. Nothing was left of Space Demons but a blank diskette and an empty box.

"You're absolutely crazy!" Ben cried. "What if it hadn't worked out like it did? What if you'd lost?"

"It was programmed to work out how it did," Andrew said nonchalantly. "There was never any *real* danger."

"I dunno," said Elaine. "We had to choose to do some pretty heavy things. Like, we had to choose to give up the gun."

"You *think* you chose," Mario said. "But what you chose was what was programmed."

Elaine opened her mouth to argue with him, but she couldn't find the words. She was trying to get her mind around the idea, but it wouldn't stand still and be grasped. It kept slipping away. They had all been forced to make choices that at the time had seemed to be tremendously difficult and painful. Had they not really had any choice at all? Had there not really been any alternative? What if they had chosen to do something quite different? Was everything that happened simply programmed to happen? She couldn't believe it.

She wanted to talk about it, but she couldn't find the right words. None of them could. Each of them looked silently around the room, avoiding the others' eyes. Inside the game they had been forced to know each other at such an intense level that it was hard to adjust to the everyday world again. They had seen a little too much of themselves and each other. They needed to get their defenses up again.

Elaine realized there was something wet on her hand. She was horribly afraid it was one of Mario's tears. Surreptitiously she wiped her hand on her skirt. Her face was growing hot. If somebody doesn't say something soon, she thought, we'll never be able to speak to each other again.

At that moment they heard footsteps outside, and the door opened. Andrew's mother surveyed the four of them with startled displeasure. The silence became even more awkward as everyone tried desperately to think of something sane and rational to say. Eventually, with idiotic brightness, Ben said, "Andrew's back! And I've finished the game."

"Yes, I can see that Andrew's back," Mrs. Hayford said drily. "Perhaps Andrew can tell me where he's been?"

Andrew was looking at his mother as though he was seeing her for the first time. He noticed how pale her face was and how much thinner she had grown. Poor Mom, he thought uncharacteristically. She looks terribly tired. He felt a sort of aching pity for her. It seemed to him that in the last few hours he had grown up irrevocably. Something had happened to him, and he was no longer a child. He thought fleetingly and wistfully of the Space Demons game. It was impossible not to be sorry it was over. It had been terrifying, but it had been so exciting and so real. And I won! he said triumphantly to himself. I did it! I got the better of it! And whatever's going to happen now, I can get the better of that too. It's funny, he reflected, I didn't know what was happening to Mom and Dad, and they didn't know what was happening to me. And they'll never know.

He gave his mother one of his charming and reassuring smiles. "We were just playing a game," he said lightly. "It was terrific!"

"There's a boy downstairs who says he's your brother," Mrs. Hayford said, looking suspiciously at Mario. "I'm not sure how he knew you were here, when I didn't know it myself, but he seems to think you'll be in trouble with your parents if you don't go home now."

"I'd better be going then," said Mario quietly. "See you, Andy! Let me know when the next game turns up."

"You bet!" Andrew said. "See you, Mars!"

"See you," Mario said politely to Mrs. Hayford. "Thanks for letting me come over!" As he ran quickly down the stairs, he saw his brother's face light up. He gave him such a hard, quick hug that John nearly missed it altogether. Then he gave him a punch in the arm, too, just to even things out. "Come on," he said. "What're we hanging around here for?" They went out the door together.

"I'd better go too," Elaine said, although she didn't know how she was ever going to get home. She was feeling weak with fatigue and relief, and the sight of Mario being so polite was almost too much for her. She was trying not to giggle, but her feelings were precarious at the moment. "Hey, Andrew!" she said, and stopped. After all they had been through together, she felt like hugging him, but she didn't think that Andrew's mother would understand.

"Yeah, what?" Andrew asked.

"Oh, nothing. See you at school."

Andrew gave her a grin, not a devastating, dazzling one, but a totally nice, no-strings-attached one, and as she and

Ben went down the stairs, he went down with them.

"Okay," he said. "Thanks, Elly."

"Thanks for what? It was all in the program, wasn't it?" she said teasingly.

"Well, thanks for being part of the program."

At the bottom of the stairs Elaine said, "I've just had a great idea! You know this show Mr. Russell wants us to put on? Well, how about the one and only, all-star, live production of *Space Demons*?"

"Starring all of us?" Ben said.

"Exactly!" Elaine was getting enthusiastic about the idea. "We could do some gymnastics and some dancing, and make it look like an electronic game, but with real people."

"Sounds great!" Ben said.

"What do you think, Andy?"

"You can't do it without me," he pointed out. "Out of all the all-stars, I was the starriest!"

"You were the villain!" Elaine said. "It was all your fault!"

"If I was the villain, who was the hero?"

"We were all heroes," she said. "We did it together."

"Even Mario?" Ben said.

"Mario was the biggest hero, in a way," Elaine said seriously. "It was hardest for him."

They stood in silence by the open front door. The evening air was fresh, but not cold; it smelled of blossoms and spring.

"Well, you'd better get going," said Andrew. He was glad they were his friends, but it was time for them to leave. "I've got to talk with my mother about something important." He could hear her footsteps coming down the stairs.

Elaine and Ben waved good night, and Andrew closed the front door and turned to face her.

"Mom," he said. "I know about Dad. He's not coming home, is he?"

When they were outside, Ben said to Elaine, "Have they really gone?"

"No," she said, "they're just up the street. We can catch them if we hurry!"

"Not them," he said. "Those dark shapes." He had been testing reality to make sure it was back to what he had always thought of as normal.

"Yeah, they've gone." She swung her head around from side to side, backward and forward. There was definitely nothing there that shouldn't be there. As she swung her head back again she did catch sight of something not normally there, but it didn't frighten her at all. It made her feel wonderfully happy.

"There's my dad!" she said.

The pickup had pulled up alongside Mario and John, just up the street. Mario had turned and was pointing in her direction. Her father jumped out of the truck, left it half in the middle of the road, and began to run toward her. The strange feeling inside her was getting stronger and stronger. When he reached her he wrapped his arms around her and gave her a bear hug.

"My God, Elly!" he said. "Where've you been? I've been so worried about you!"

Worried about me? she thought. He was actually worried about me? Then she remembered that they'd had a fight, and that she'd hardly spoken to him since. It was dark and he hadn't known where she was. She had a great feeling of relief, followed by a glimmering of how awful it would have been if he hadn't missed her and hadn't worried about her. The strange feeling completely overwhelmed her. "Oh, no!" she said. "I think I'm going to cry!"

Ben had already gone down the street to join Mario, and Elaine got into the pickup. Under the front seat she found a box of tissues. Somebody had stepped on it, crushing the box and leaving a bootprint on it, and dust lay thick on the top tissue, but the ones underneath were quite serviceable. Elaine used them to dry her eyes and blow her nose.

After a moment her father said, "I thought you'd run away from home!"

"How could I?" she replied tartly. "We don't have a home for me to run away from!" She was beginning to feel extraordinarily punchy again, as though she could take on anybody or anything. "I'm starving," she said. "Let's go and get something to eat."

He turned on the ignition and put the truck in gear. "Shall we pick up the guys?" he said as they approached Mario and John, who had started to cycle home, with Ben on the back of Mario's bike.

"No, not now!" Elaine said. "I've had enough of boys for today!"

David honked the horn and waved to them as they drove past. "Haven't you made friends with any girls at school?" he asked.

"I don't seem to have the knack for it," Elaine said. "But I might give it another try. I've got someone in mind." Her good feeling extended even to Linda. I'll talk to Linda tomorrow, she promised herself. I'll ask her to be in our show. I really will try to be friends.

"It wouldn't be a bad idea for you to know some more girls, you know," her father said. There was a short pause, and then he went on, "I had a talk with your teacher after school."

Elaine was immediately alert. Something was up. He never usually asked questions about who her friends were, and he was choosing his words too carefully.

"What about?" she asked guardedly.

Her father changed tack again. "I worry about you sometimes, Elly. I wonder if it's much of a life for you, just tagging along after me."

Since this was pretty much what she'd been wondering herself lately, she said nothing. They stopped at a red light. She took a quick look at his face. Under the orange street lights it was a very curious color. His forehead was creased and his eyes were sad. An extremely painful feeling hit her in the stomach and made her eyes prick with tears again. She stared hard out the window as the light turned green and they moved forward again. "Don't worry about me," she said. "I'll probably be all right."

Her father put out a hand and took hers. Then he said with a rush, as if he was trying to get it all over with at once, "Peter Russell thinks it would be a bad idea for you to change schools again this year. He says Mrs. Fields is hoping to find another foster child to move in with them. How would you feel about staying with her till the end of the year?"

"Where would you be?" Elaine said. Her heart had started to pound, but she wasn't sure whether it was because of fear, or what.

"Well, I'd get work down south and save up some money, and then I'd come back for Christmas."

Elaine swallowed hard. Two conflicting emotions were raging in her mind: relief that she would be able to stay on at Kingsgate; panic that her father might be wanting to get rid of her.

"Don't you want me to come with you?" she asked.

"Of *course* I do!" He said it with such force that she knew it was true. "I'd much rather have you with me. But I want to do what's best for you. It's not much of a life for a kid, always on the move like this, especially now that you're growing up. You need someone who'll look after you properly."

"Does Mrs. Fields want to have me?"

"Peter seemed pretty certain she would. I wanted to find out how you felt first."

"I don't know how I feel," she said. She only knew that she felt completely overwhelmed. "I'll have to think about it."

"I want you to make up your own mind," he said. "I want you to choose what *you* want to do. I'll go along with that."

Yes, I can do that, she thought. I can choose. I don't know yet what I will choose, but whatever choice I make, it'll work out. And this way, if I do move on, it'll be because *I* choose to, not because someone else is bulldozing me into it.

She gave her father a grin. She felt full of optimism about the future.

Dear Mom, she wrote in her mind. *This is the last letter you'll ever get from me. I am signing off now. Just thought you'd like to know—I'm going to make it without you!*

Love and kisses from Elaine Taylor.

About the Author

Gillian Rubinstein originally wrote this book for her son, who she says "was fascinated by computer games—and I was fascinated by the kids who play them." She was born in England and was graduated from Oxford University. She now lives with her husband and three children in Lynton, South Australia, and is writing a sequel to *Space Demons*.

RUB   Rubinstein, Gillian
  C1   Space demons

$13.95

	DATE